In 1934, almost everyone struggles to pay the rent, and Alex Dawson is no exception. To support his writing habit, he moonlights with his mentor Donnie as a bodyguard for the mayor. It's dull work, until the night a handsome, golden-eyed stranger catches his eye—and both his boss and his mentor are killed when his back is turned.

Jobless and emotionally adrift, Alex vows to find the murderer before the corrupt police can pin the blame on him. But he soon discovers he's in over his head. The golden-eyed stranger turns out to be a mob boss's cousin, and a suspicious stack of money in Donnie's dresser leads Alex to discover that his mentor and the mayor were involved in something more crooked than fundraising dinners and campaign speeches. As the death count rises amid corruption, mob politics, and anarchist plots, Alex realizes that the murders aren't political or even business. This is the work of a spree killer, and Alex and his new boyfriend are the only ones who can stop them.

No Good Men

The Caro Mysteries, Book One

Thea McAlistair

A NineStar Press Publication

Published by NineStar Press
P.O. Box 91792,
Albuquerque, New Mexico, 87199 USA.
www.ninestarpress.com

No Good Men

Printed in the USA
First Edition
September, 2019

Print ISBN: 978-1-951057-37-4

Also available in eBook, ISBN: 978-1-951057-36-7

Warning: This book contains violence & gore, a character death, police brutality, homophobia, and mentions of racism, sex work, and domestic abuse.

To my grandfather and my middle school English teacher, who encouraged the stories.

Chapter One

MOB MONEY COULD buy a lot, but apparently it couldn't buy taste. Every single architectural detail of the Ostia struck me as garish: from the chandeliers dripping crystals to the thick wooden accent panels to the gold-painted cherubs carved into the tops of the columns. But my opinion didn't matter; I was just hired muscle.

The club had opened the previous December—about two seconds after booze turned legal again—and attracted all sorts of upper-class clientele, including my boss, Mayor Roy Carlisle. They called him the White Knight of Westwick, and he ran on the rather ironic platform of driving various ne'er-do-wells out of the city. But again, not my business. My job was to hover just behind him in case something terrible happened. Nothing ever happened though, no crazed attackers or falling pianos. The worst crisis I'd run into in the ten or so months I'd been working for him was a freak rainstorm at a garden party, and I had to hold my jacket over his wife Emma's head to protect her hair.

Still, it was a dollar a night to stand around, and that was more than other people were getting. The Depression had wiped everyone out, including me. If I hadn't taken up bodyguarding, I would've been thrown out of my room in the boardinghouse faster than I could say eviction. Writing pulp stories wasn't a lucrative day job, and even less so at the beginning of a career.

Which was why, despite my thoughts on the decor, I was pleased to be at the Ostia. Everyone said they had the best acts in town, and I couldn't disagree. That night they opened with a pretty, button-nosed redhead. She was French, or at least she had a good enough grip of the language to sing in it. I didn't know what she was singing about, but it sounded sultry enough as she made eyes at our table.

Carlisle lapped it up, ignorant or indifferent to Emma turning bright pink beside him. She didn't say anything though. Maybe she'd taken a lesson from other political wives and learned to swallow her pride or risk becoming divorced and destitute. Not that she didn't deserve to be proud. She was thirty-five—ten years Carlisle's junior—pretty, blonde, and delicate with huge blue eyes.

She must have gotten her looks from her mother, because her father had the smashed face of a bulldog and towered over even my own six feet. Seated to his daughter's left that night, Marc Logan also stewed in silence, his hand alternately crumpling the napkins and patting Emma reassuringly on the knee. His own blue eyes, the haunting color of old ice, bored a hole into the side of Carlisle's head.

Their dinner guest for the evening, their neighbor Mrs. Green, likewise noticed his glare and apparently decided the best course of action was distraction. "Emma dear, did you see what Miss Kepler was wearing the other night at the Peterson soiree?" she tittered as she coiled the chain for her hanging glasses around a finger.

"Hmm?" Emma turned her head just enough to keep her husband in her peripheral vision. "I'm sorry; what were you saying about the Kepler girl?"

"Her dress!" exclaimed Mrs. Green. "It was scandalous! So low-cut. Anyone would have thought she was selling herself. Her father should never have let her out of the house like that. Don't you agree, Mr. Logan?"

Logan blinked slowly, no doubt trying to come to terms with the dullness of a conversation centered on someone else's clothing. "While I have to agree that she was... improperly dressed for the occasion, it is quite difficult for a man to say no to his daughter once she's gotten her mind wrapped around something." He glanced at Emma, who smiled weakly.

Mrs. Green continued along the thread of scandalous attire, but I let my attention slip back to Carlisle. Oblivious to the rest of his table, he continued to stare at the French singer. While such behavior wasn't unusual for him, that night it was so obvious that even I was becoming uncomfortable. I glanced at my watch and suppressed a groan. It was only half-past ten. Donnie wouldn't be around for another hour and a half.

"Are you feeling all right, Mr. Dawson?"

My attention snapped to Emma. "Yes, ma'am," I answered, hoping she hadn't noticed my boredom.

Her mouth quirked like she was in on some joke I didn't know the punchline to, but she said nothing else. Instead she turned to her father, placed a hand on his shoulder, and whispered something in his ear. He grunted in response. Carlisle didn't notice the exchange, or maybe didn't care. Mrs. Green kept nattering away.

The song stopped, and the French girl took a bow. We all clapped, Carlisle too enthusiastically, and Emma barely at all. The girl swept off the stage to a table off the wing for a break, and she was replaced by a dark-haired woman with too much makeup. The new woman sang with a rough alto voice, occasionally throwing appraising looks at Carlisle, though he didn't return them. Once the French girl left, his attention had returned to the food. The rest of the table did the same.

With my charges occupied, I took the chance to look over the room again. Nothing out of the ordinary. Diners, waiters, a glossy bar at the back. The maître-de waving through a man who had just entered... I realized I knew the man weaving his way between tables. Donnie was terribly noticeable with a thick, out-of-fashion beard and pocket-watch chain draped across his waistcoat. I looked at my own watch again. It was only eleven.

"How's it going, Alex?" Donnie asked as he took up a place beside me.

"What are you doing here so early?" I whispered.

"Early, you say?" He rubbed at his beard thoughtfully. Too thoughtfully. Then he winked and chuckled.

I squinted at him. Whatever Donnie was here for, it wasn't because he'd miscalculated. He was precise, so precise that he'd been a watchmaker before the stock market crashed and ruined the market for luxury goods. Then he'd taken a series of jobs burly men normally take—lumber yard, bricklaying—before landing the night bodyguarding job, where he ended up thriving. He could deal with the tedium of long stretches of nothing, but also had the brains to handle any emergency that might come up. I was flattered to hear that when Logan had asked for another guard for Carlisle with the same traits, Donnie had offered my name.

Donnie had always been too good to me. He'd been a friend of my dad's, and all but adopted me after the alcoholic bastard poisoned himself with white lightning eight years ago in '26. Kept me in school, even. I was lucky he had, because no one else would have taken on a fourteen-year-old with a police record.

"Mr. Kemp!" Carlisle exclaimed. "Is it midnight already?" He reached for his own watch. "Ah, no, not even close."

Donnie half bowed. "Forgive me, sir. I'm just very excited to be at such a fine place."

Something was going on, and I wasn't in the loop. I made a mental note to have a chat with Donnie later about how he was too old to tease people and get away with it for long.

"I don't blame you. It *is* very fine," Carlisle answered, throwing a look at the French girl, who was still on break at one of the nearby tables. She winked back. Emma found something on the tablecloth to study. Carlisle scanned over me and Donnie. "But I'm only paying one of you, so you and Mr. Dawson are going to have to fight it out between yourselves."

I tried to do the numbers in my head. As desperately as I wanted to leave, an hour's work was a good fifteen cents, and fifteen cents could go a long way. Food, coffee, cigarettes if I bought the cheap kind.

"Eh, just pay the boy his regular wages. He's young. Let him have some fun." Donnie smiled and nudged me in the ribs. My face flushed.

Carlisle laughed. "You're too soft-hearted, Kemp. But how does anyone say no to such solid reasoning? Here." He fished some nickels out of a pocket and handed them to me. "One night of double pay won't kill me. Just don't make it a habit. I can't be doing this for the next four years!"

"You've only just announced that you're running again, Roy," mumbled Emma.

Carlisle kept smiling. "Don't be so pessimistic. I'm a shoe-in. Their knight in shining armor, remember? You can't beat that."

"Tides turn," said Emma. "The public is fickle."

He snorted and waved a dismissive hand. Then he turned his attention back to me. "Don't listen to her. Women don't know anything about politics. Silly creatures."

Emma closed her eyes, her jaw clenched.

I took the nickels and got out of there. I never knew if Carlisle baited her on purpose or if he was just that dim, though after months of shadowing him for six hours a day, I suspected it was the latter. How he'd gotten himself through law school and then elected mayor was anyone's guess. My money was on either Emma or Logan having done all the hard work.

It would have been a shame to be in the Ostia and not have at least a drink, so I took a detour to the bar in the back on my way out. I ordered a cheap beer. The bartender looked me over once before getting it. I tugged at my jacket. I knew I didn't look swanky enough for the place. My navy suit was fraying at the cuffs, and there were flecked ink stains on my tie that wouldn't come out no matter how hard I scrubbed.

In defiance of his attitude, I took my time drinking and listening to the singer belt out heartbreaking songs about lovers leaving. I couldn't see her from my seat in the back, but I could still picture her in my mind's eye. I started mentally writing a story about her, and when it got to be too long of a thread, I pulled the notepad out of my pocket. I'd scribbled about a page and a half when someone sat next to me.

I glanced at him. He wore a grayish-green suit and had brown, curly hair oiled back so tightly that it was practically smooth. He pulled out a silver cigarette case. I dropped my eyes back to my notebook.

"Would you like one?" he asked. A whisper of an accent I couldn't identify tugged at the edge of his words, deepening and rounding the vowels.

I raised my head. He held the case out to me, his own cigarette perched in a smirk. I hesitated. I didn't like handouts, and they were poorly rolled, but I'd used up the last of my own the day before, and I wasn't about to waste money on the expensive ones the girls of the Ostia were shilling.

"Yeah, okay," I said as I took one. "Thanks."

His smirk turned into a full smile, and the corners of his eyes crinkled into crows-feet. How old was he? He had at least half a dozen years on me. Thirty? Thirty-five? Though he had the air of someone older. Maybe it was the scar running vertically on his left cheek, or maybe it was something about his eyes. They were such a light brown they were almost gold. Yeah, that was it. Golden eyes like a weathered immortal. I returned to my notebook to scratch that one down before I forgot it.

"You know, it helps if you light it," he said.

"Oh, yeah. Heh." I reached for my lighter, but he already had his out. With a flick of a finger, the flame appeared against the edge of the cigarette hanging from my mouth. I blushed, unaccustomed to attention from handsome men. Women, yes, occasionally—a particularly brazen one once told me I had a jawline sharp enough to cut herself on—but somehow I'd never attracted the right sort of guy. Maybe they thought I was too intimidating with my height and broad shoulders.

"Well at least I'm not barking up the wrong tree today," he said. He took a long drag on his own cigarette. "May I ask what you're writing?"

I closed my notebook. "Nothing important. Just... ideas for stories."

"You're a writer?"

Could I call myself a writer when the only things I'd sold were a couple of pulp shorts and a dime romance that had been split apart and edited so much that it was barely mine anymore? What if he asked what I'd written and I told him and he didn't know? Or worse, he *did* know?

"I have aspirations," I answered.

"Those are good things to have." He leaned forward, and his smoky breath cascaded around my ear and my neck, sending lightning down my spine. "I have some too."

My thoughts raced almost as fast as my heartbeat. This had mistake written all over it. Best case scenario, I was about to be used. Worst case, some kind of set-up. I'd been caught in one of them before, and I'd sworn I would know better next time. But then, what was life without a little risk? Unable to make a decision, I stalled.

"And what are your aspirations, mister...?"

He offered his hand. "Forgive me. My name is—"

Two pops cut off the rest. Gunfire.

I leaped up, my stomach plunging to my feet. Several women screamed. I shoved my way back to the table through the panicking and scrambling patrons.

Roy Carlisle was dead. I knew it before I even got to the table. He was sprawled out facedown, missing half his head. The other half was spattered across the surroundings. Emma sat in the chair next to him, blinking in shocked silence at the brains and blood sprayed all over her. Donnie was nowhere to be seen.

"Donnie?" I shouted as I stumbled between the last few tables.

I nearly tripped over him. He had taken a bullet to the chest, blood spilling out of his mouth into his beard. His mouth moved, but only bubbly gasps came out. The world shrank. Before I knew it, I was on the floor, trying in futile desperation to cover the wound with my hands and fallen napkins. His chest heaved once, twice, then stopped moving entirely. I looked at his face, hoping to see some kind of spark, but there was nothing. His head lolled to the side, his eyes blank.

Suddenly Logan hauled me up by the back of my jacket and shook me like a puppy. "Get a grip on yourself, man. For God's sake."

It was only then that I realized I was bawling. I went to wipe my eyes, but I stopped when I noticed that my hands were covered in blood. Donnie's blood, all over my cuffs, pooling under Logan's shoes. I gagged, and Logan shook me again.

"I said pull yourself together," he growled.

Breathe. That was what Donnie had always told me. If I was losing myself, I should just breathe. Everything else would fall into place. So I sucked in some air and let it go, over and over, while I listened to the sirens getting closer.

Chapter Two

DETECTIVE HARLOW SHUT the door of the interview room and tossed a bunch of files onto the table before sitting across from me. My heart raced, making the pounding in my head all the worse. I had no idea why I'd been pulled in for questioning when there were literally dozens of other people who had witnessed the murder. Like I'd told the cops at least three times before Harlow showed up and dragged me into the station, I'd been oblivious on the other side of the room.

Harlow was an older man, with a beer gut and thin hair on top going from black to gray, but he still had hands like knotted oak roots. I could tell already he was one of those cops who closed cases, and not in a clever Sherlock-Holmes kind of way. I hoped I had a sufficiently neutral look on my face. If Harlow decided he didn't like me for whatever reason, I might end the night missing a tooth on top of everything else.

He flipped open one of the files. "Alexander Dawson," he read aloud. "Age, twenty-three. Occupation, writer—freelance. Bodyguard—also freelance." He looked up at me with one eyebrow cocked like he expected me to account for something.

I shrugged. "Keeps me off the breadline."

He didn't respond and instead went back to reading my police record. "Assault, 1925. Assault, 1927." He raised his head again.

I met his eyes steadily. They were both juvenile charges, more for brawling than anything really dangerous. I'd imitated my father's actions on my classmates. But Donnie had persuaded me that I was better than that. Not that I didn't still have a temper, but at least now it was constructively aimed. I braced myself for what I knew he was going to say next.

Harlow continued, "And gross indecency, 1932."

I resisted rolling my eyes. My love life, illegal or not, was unrelated to murder. "Did you pull me in just because I have a record? A record, I might add, that has nothing to do with what happened tonight."

Harlow flipped my file shut and opened another one. "Funny thing is, your old pal Donald Kemp has the same charge. Different year though. Back in the twenties. I'm almost surprised. You could practically spit in God's eye without consequence back in those days."

Same charge? He couldn't be talking about the violence; Donnie'd never have hurt a fly. *But then that would mean...* Suddenly everything he'd ever done to protect me made a lot more sense. A fresh wave of grief flooded through me, but I tamped it down.

"I still don't know what any of this has to do with Mayor Carlisle's assassination," I said.

"Maybe it does, maybe it doesn't. We're just asking questions right now."

"Well my answer's the same: I didn't see anything. I was writing at the bar. Not even looking until after I heard the shots."

"Kind of convenient, don't you think? You being as far away from the stage as possible?"

I leaned forward. "I know what you're doing. You don't have anything to work with, so you just grabbed everyone who was there who has a record, hoping that somebody squawks about some other crime so you can make an arrest and not look incompeten—"

Harlow's hand shot out and gripped my hair before shoving me face-first into the tabletop. Pain exploded from my nose to behind my eyes, forcing tears out of them. I swore as he let go, more at myself for not keeping a check on my big mouth than from the actual injury. Blood welled inside my nose, and I scrambled for a handkerchief.

"So you were at the bar," Harlow continued gently, like he hadn't just tried to smash my face in. "Can anyone corroborate that?"

I debated what I could say as blood seeped into my handkerchief and down the back of my throat. Saying nothing might get me worse than a banged up nose. Saying yes might get me out of there, but it also might get me some kind of solicitation charge. But solicitation was better than murder, right? "Yes. There was... a man there. Slicked brown hair, gray suit. Trim. Little shorter than average." *Golden eyes.* "He asked about my newest book."

"Did you happen to catch his name?"

I realized I hadn't. "No." I didn't know if I felt lucky or not. They might not be able to hunt him down if they didn't know his name, but then, I wouldn't be able to either. The memory of his hot breath on my neck flashed and faded.

"Well it's a good thing I already have his name," said Harlow. He switched to yet another file, this one much thicker than the other two. "Severo Argenti. And we have him right outside waiting his turn."

"What?" I blurted it before I could stop myself.

But who wouldn't have exclaimed over that? Everyone knew Severo Argenti was a cousin of the Queen of Sin herself, Bella Bellissima, and maybe her best contract killer. The papers all said he was a vicious murderer who'd knife a person as soon as look at them, but the man I had met was soft-spoken and had a charming smile. Not to say he couldn't be all those things, but the images didn't mesh well in my head. And anyway, I couldn't imagine some mob goon being, well, like me.

I guess my shock surprised Harlow because his brow scrunched for a moment. But he smoothed it out and kept going. "So you claim you don't know him."

"I did not know the man at the bar with me was Severo Argenti," I said clearly for the benefit of anyone who was listening in.

Harlow's mouth twisted for a moment. Thinking, probably. Generally, Neanderthals like that need to take their time changing directions when things aren't going to plan. "Would you say he was a distraction?"

"A distraction?" *Yes, he was one hell of a distraction.* "I don't understand."

"Did he distract you from doing your job?"

I chanced taking the handkerchief away from my nose. It had stopped bleeding, but I could still feel it congealing inside. "I was already off for the night. Donald Kemp came early, and Mr. Carlisle dismissed me. You can ask anyone at that table." *Well, except for Donnie and Carlisle.*

Harlow's eyes tracked across my face. I didn't know what he expected to see. Evidence of lying? Wondering what a gangster saw in me? Or maybe he was just taking in my bruised nose as evidence that he'd already tried violence to make me talk.

He crossed his arms. "All right, Dawson, get out. But don't go skipping town. We may have more questions to ask you."

I didn't need telling twice. I grabbed my hat and jacket from behind my chair and got the hell out of the interview room before he could change his mind.

The hall buzzed with activity. It was only to be expected. Someone had offed the mayor—the mayor who had based his campaign on stamping out organized crime—in front of a hundred possible witnesses. But would anything actually get solved? Corruption was rampant, and not least in the police department. There were any number of deep-pocketed people in town who could stall an investigation until it went cold or even silence people entirely. I sighed in disappointment. No justice for Carlisle meant no justice for Donnie.

"Move!" snapped an officer as he shoved me against a wall.

By the time I'd bounced against it with a curse on my lips, he was already several yards away, hustling a handcuffed man to the interview room I'd just left. I shouted after him anyway. "Watch where you're going, jackass!"

He ignored me, but the prisoner he was escorting turned his head. Golden eyes. Severo Argenti. My mouth fell open, but nothing came out, and before I could try again, the door slammed after him.

I SHOVED OPEN the station door, and the sunlight nearly blinded me. I'd been held up in the station for the whole night and most of the morning. Friday morning. I had to keep telling myself it had been less than twelve hours since the murders. I wandered back home, moving on muscle memory alone. The coppery smell of blood permeated my every breath.

"Alex?"

The world came into focus again. I was in one of the alleys that ran behind the fenced rows of houses. Through the nearest gate I could see the fading yard of a blue-painted, crumbling duplex. Martin's house, or what was left of it after he'd run out of savings. Had I made it so far into my neighborhood already? Martin himself stood on his back porch, basket of laundry in hand. Say anything about the dilapidated building, but he kept everything clean.

"Alex, what happened?" he exclaimed.

It was only then that I thought about how I must look. Bruises, blood, and God-knew what else. "It's fine," I said. The back of my throat burned when I spoke. "I'm fine." Suddenly the world seemed tipsy. I leaned against the fence for support as everything washed through me.

Donnie's dead. Donnie's dead. Donnie's dead.

Martin abandoned his basket and ran down the stairs and out the gate. He took a hold of my arm and draped it around his shoulder. I hesitated about letting him take any of my weight—he was skinny as a rail, after all—but I had no choice. He all but carried me into the kitchen and dumped me into a chair.

It was quite a pretty place to have a complete breakdown. Afternoon light poured through the window above the sink and onto the polished floor. A green plaid tablecloth draped and tucked over his table, which was topped by a chipped vase filled with white irises. The flowers were likely a thank-you gift from a neighbor, since Martin didn't go in for gardening such frivolous things as inedible plants.

"Don't move," he said before he disappeared into the hallway. He came back a few seconds later with a blanket and draped it across my shoulders. "What happened?" he repeated as he ran water into a glass for me. I would have preferred something stiffer, but as far as I knew, Martin drank even less than I did.

I slumped against the table and pressed the glass against my aching face. The coolness brought me back to myself. "Donnie's dead," I managed to croak. "And Mayor Carlisle."

"I saw; it was in the papers this morning." Martin's eyes widened as he made the connection. "You were there! Oh my God, Alex, you need to talk to the police–"

"I spent all night with the police. And they gave me this." I straightened and pointed at my bruised nose. "And I'm going to tell you what I told everyone else. I. Saw. Nothing!"

Martin nodded and swallowed but didn't say anything. I felt bad for my outburst. Now that I was looking, he seemed worse for wear himself. His cheeks were covered in about two days' worth of stubble, and his already-rheumy eyes had bags under them.

"Sorry," I mumbled. "Didn't mean to shout."

"Apology accepted. I've had worse said to me anyway." He turned to the cabinets and started shuffling through the mostly bare shelves. "Do you want something to eat? I imagine they didn't give you any food or water at the police station."

They hadn't, in fact. Which meant I hadn't had anything resembling a meal since dinner on Wednesday, having skipped lunch yesterday to stretch my budget. No wonder I was dizzy. I chugged the water, and it washed some of the metallic taste from my mouth. When I set the glass down, I saw that Martin was slicing up some bread. It was pretty obviously the end of a stale loaf, but it was good of him to share. He didn't bother with a plate, which was fine, because I didn't need one. I gulped it down almost as fast as the water.

He frowned. "I'd offer you more, but..."

"No, it's fine. That was plenty," I answered, ignoring how the little bit of food made me realize how hungry I really was.

He sat in the chair across from me. "Do you think John Rutherford had something to do with the killing?"

I drew a blank for a moment before remembering Rutherford was Carlisle's opponent in the upcoming mayoral race. I was so used to hearing him called "Rolling Rutherford," his bulldozers plowing through neighborhoods in the name of development and progress. His people had sniffed around the area a few months ago, searching for anyone who could be convinced to sell in order to make way for a department store and associated parking lot. Most, like Martin and my landlord, had refused, and the men went away again. Not long after, Rutherford threw his hat into the ring.

"Oh I don't know," I grumbled. "If he did, I bet the cops'll grab him in no time."

Martin snorted and rolled his eyes. I shrugged. I didn't entirely believe it myself, but I had to put *some* faith in the justice of the universe right then or else I was going to lose it. As it was, I was still feeling the effects of having my face smashed and my father-figure killed in front of me. The edge of my vision blurred every time I moved.

"I think you should stay here for a little while," Martin said as he studied my face. "You look like you're going to pass out."

I shook my head. "No, I should..." What should I be doing? My brain was a scramble. Instinctively, I went to the answer I always had for myself: I should be writing. I reached for my notebook. But it wasn't in my pocket. Several months' worth of ideas gone. The additional loss was too much. I put my head down on the table again so Martin wouldn't see the tears welling up.

I didn't see him leave, but he must have, because the next thing I knew, he dropped something heavy next to my face. I jolted up. It was a doctor's bag so big I wouldn't have thought he could lift it.

Martin had once been a surgeon at the big hospital downtown. But that had been almost ten years back. I'd heard lots of rumors about why he had been sacked, and they were all different. He'd killed a patient. He'd been caught with another man's wife. He'd performed terminations. He'd threatened the director. The list of possibilities went on forever. I'd never asked for the truth because I was afraid what the answer might be.

He rooted through the bag for a few moments, then pulled out a small bottle rattling with pills. He poured out two and went to hand them to me. I shied away.

"I don't want to be sedated," I said. What if the drugs fogged up my memory? I might forget the moments before Donnie died, when he smiled as he let me take money right from under him. And if the police came after me again, I'd be as helpless as a lump of old gum.

"It's for the greater good, my friend," Martin answered as he pressed them into my hand. "You'll thank me in a few hours."

I caved, mostly because I didn't want to feel the soreness in my face anymore, and took the pills with the last swig of water in the glass. Once I did, he cajoled me into the living room. I settled on the couch and was struck by how soft it felt. I blinked, and my eyelids felt like they were a hundred pounds. I knew pills couldn't work that fast, but my body, now that it had the option, was giving out. And it wasn't like Martin was going to poison me or anything. So I let go and let the darkness swallow me.

Chapter Three

SOMETHING SLAMMED, AND I flinched awake at the sound, imagining gunshots again. But it was just the screen door that had banged open. It took me a few blinks to realize who had come in. All I could see through the haze was a blur of black and beige and orange.

"Hi, Mr. Dawson. What are you doing here?"

I recognized the voice. It was only Pearl Taggart and her calico cat Daisy. The girl was six, the cat somewhat older than that, and they were both practically feral. Her dad was a drunk and her mom had run off ages ago, so more often than not, she wandered around the streets with her pet. The near parallel to my own childhood gave me a soft spot for her, but Martin played the fathering part that Donnie had for me. I had no idea what was going to happen when she got older, but the situation worked for the time being.

"I could ask you the same question," I grumbled as I tried to sit up. The neatly arranged room pitched sideways and dragged my stomach with it. If I had been dizzy before, it was nothing compared to now. Dried blood crackled inside my nose. "Shouldn't you be in school or something?"

"It's over for the day."

Was it that late already? I must have been out for hours. I nodded, careful not to move too fast in case I got queasier or set my nose bleeding again. I looked away from Pearl, focusing on the solid brass base of the nearest lamp, hoping the room would steady and she would go away.

She either didn't realize I was ignoring her or took it as a challenge. She waved the cat in my face. It growled and swished its tail in response. "Daisy hurt her paw," she declared.

I chanced glancing at the cat's foot. Something had scraped the fur off, but there was no blood. I found I had no sympathy for such a pathetic injury.

Martin hurried in from his den. "Pearl! Now is not the time." He tried to shoo her back into the kitchen, but she evaded him.

"I heard Mr. Dawson's friend died. The one with the beard. Mr. Kemp." She stroked the cat, her too-big eyes peering at me from under greasy bangs. They were green and bulgy, like search lamps picking up everything around her. "I'm sorry."

"Yeah, me too," I answered. "But thanks."

"I mean it, Pearl," insisted Martin. "Go home. Mr. Dawson needs to rest."

"I'm all right." To prove the point, I struggled to my feet. To my surprise, I was able to stand without tilting. "I'm just gonna go home if it's all the same to you."

He frowned. "I don't recommend it, but I can't stop you."

Pearl squeaked and let Daisy leap out of her arms. The cat bolted back for the kitchen door as the girl latched on to my hand. "Walk me home! Sometimes the other kids throw rocks at me if I'm by myself."

How could I say no to that? And anyway, it was better if I wasn't alone. What if the sedatives kicked back in and I passed out in the street? If being woken up on Martin's couch was bad, I could only imagine what it would be like in a drunk tank.

The sun was much lower than it had been on my way back from the police station, and it sent long gray shadows across what was left of the pavement. It had been a nice area once, a middle-class neighborhood halfway between downtown and the mansions on the hill that overlooked the Westwick River. The houses with yards, solid brownstones, and small shops had been something of a shock for me when I moved out of my father's tin-roofed slum shanty into Donnie's apartment.

It seemed the slum had followed me though. Only a few months after I found my own place to live, the stocks dropped, and the middle-class neighborhood I'd grown to love steadily lost its glamor. Most of the main road was pocked with ruts, ignored by city repairmen for over three years. It was just as well. There weren't too many cars left, and those were already shaky. The tall houses I'd been so impressed by were abandoned by their struggling occupants and left to succumb to the elements, their once-green lawns brown and overgrown. Several winters of strong storms ripped off shingles and siding, and summers of humid heat peeled the paint. The people who remained, like Martin, tried their best, but even they couldn't compete with Mother Nature.

Pearl and I only made it a block before I saw Vern Temple. He leaned against a lamppost and chewed on a toothpick like he was some kind of thug and not a five-foot-four reporter pushing fifty. He flashed a brilliant smile, teeth stark white in his dark complexion. Likely he was aiming for charming, but the impression I got was of a shark sizing up his kill. His observant gaze raked across my bruised face and bloodied clothes.

"Cute kid," he called. "She yours?"

I groaned. I was far too lightheaded for this. Vern was as yellow a journalist as they came, and he looked the part too. His hat was always on crooked and his tie always halfway undone. He favored light-colored suits and, more often than not, had the jacket slung over his shoulder. He made regular rounds at Carlisle's offices looking for stories, and I'd had to throw him out more than once for being too much of a nuisance. He always came after me because he knew I was a writer and would at least listen to him. Not many people would even do that based on his brown skin alone.

"Little busy today, sorry," I said as flatly as I could.

"Yeah, I heard." He pushed himself off the wall. "Damn shame about Mr. Kemp. And Mr. Carlisle, of course."

I shoved Pearl along, hoping she would take the hint and start moving faster. "Why don't you bother the coroner, Vern? Or the police? I'm sure they've got something for you to scribble about by now."

"You believe they won't talk to a single reporter? Said it's 'an ongoing investigation.' Since when has that ever stopped them?"

"Well, you know, it *is* the mayor who's dead. Even they know they need a little decorum."

Pearl stopped in her tracks, and I nearly tripped over her. "What's decorum mean?"

"It means being polite," I answered. I gave Vern a hard stare. "It's why we don't speak ill of the dead."

Vern shrugged but didn't say anything. If Vern was good at one thing, it was finding connections where no one else saw them. Sometimes they were real, and sometimes they were entirely made up. As far as I knew, he understood the difference, but couldn't care less as long as it sold papers. Was he concocting some story in his head to use if I decided to stay silent? And if he was, would Donnie be on the wrong side of it? Would *I* be on the wrong side of it?

"All right, just... wait for me at my boardinghouse," I said. "I'll be there in ten minutes."

Vern winked. "Knew you'd come through for me, Dawson."

He tossed the toothpick into the gutter and strolled in the direction of my place. I watched him for a few seconds to make sure he wasn't about to turn around and start following me instead.

Pearl tugged on my sleeve. "I know him!"

"Yeah?" What could Vern want with a little girl? I hoped it was something simple like bribing her with candy to tell about a lead and not anything more twisted. "From where?"

"He comes around to Daddy's work sometimes."

I sighed in relief. At least that was one piece of good luck today. Bert Taggart's "work" was as a two-bit boxer who spent a lot of his time in a crumbling gymnasium that had once been a somewhat less-crumbling warehouse. Whether he actually did any training was a different issue, but it made more sense for Vern to be sniffing out scandal there than in the neighborhood.

Pearl's house was empty, so I felt all right leaving her there. She wasn't a destructive kid and kept herself out of trouble for the most part. If her father had been in, I would have stayed at least for a little while, just to make sure he was in an amicable mood. I'd been belted enough times that I'd never forget the sting, and I couldn't imagine the same thing happening to a frail kid like Pearl.

Vern was waiting next to the stoop of my boardinghouse, as agreed. His beige suit was almost the same color as the sandstone walls. He grinned again. "So, anything you want to tell your old pal Vern?"

I thought about making something up, but I didn't want to stoop to his level. "I'll tell you what I told the police. I was on the other side of the room, back to the shooter. I didn't see anything."

"You were there though. Bet you saw plenty of stuff before you conveniently turned around."

Memories of Carlisle and his wife's tiff flickered through my head. But she hadn't been the one to shoot him, certainly. And anyway, that was normal marriage stuff. At least, that was what I'd heard. I shrugged. "Even if I had, I don't remember."

"Yeah, and I bet the cops believed that too."

I shook my head. I should have known he wouldn't have been deterred. But I was starting to get annoyed, and my ongoing faintness wasn't helping. "They should because it's the truth. And don't you start any rumors. Donnie Kemp was a good man."

Vern laughed. It was a rough sound like bricks being scraped together. "There aren't any good men. Just men who keep skeletons in closets."

His words resonated through me. "You're a cynical bastard, aren't you?"

"I prefer the term realist." He shook his head and gave me a pitying look. "So what's yours?"

"My what?"

"Skeleton. There's something fishy about you, my friend, and when I figure out—"

Before I knew I was doing it, I slammed him against the wall of the building. He grimaced as his back hit the stone, but he stared me dead in the eye as he said, "Temper, Dawson. You want to be pulled in for assault again?"

All my rage morphed into fear, and I let go of him. Had he seen my police record? When? Had he been planning this long in advance, holding his trump card until the best moment? Or was he goading me, making up stories and hoping I'd bite like he did with his editors?

Vern bent down to retrieve his hat. "Look at you, all pale! What, you never hit a reporter before? I thought that was first-blood for bodyguards."

I glanced around to see if anyone had witnessed what had happened between us, but the street was deserted. I rubbed my sweating palms on my thighs. "I was... I just pushed you is all."

"Well then, you understand why I've got to do a little pushing of my own." He adjusted his jacket. "Give me something or I get it around that you're queer."

I'd always known blackmail was on my horizon since my youthful indiscretions were a matter of public record, but I hadn't expected it to happen until I was older, living the good life from publishing royalties. At least my theoretical future self had money to pay people off with. "But I don't know anything!" I insisted.

"Well, chat up the wife. You worked for them. You can talk to her without it becoming a problem. And we don't want *problems*, do we?"

It was swallow my pride or never work in town again. I didn't have a choice. "Fine, okay, you win. I'll poke at somebody for you."

"Good man." Vern flicked out a business card. "That's my office phone. If I'm not there, keep trying." He shook my hand aggressively. "And if I didn't say it before, my condolences, Alex."

He nodded once, then wandered off down the street. I shoved his card in my pocket. What would happen if I couldn't deliver? I tore my mind up trying to think of ways last night hadn't been just like every other night, something that would placate the police and now Vern. But nothing caught. I just saw the way Donnie's mouth opened and closed like a fish's. And who was I in that scene? The idiot who did too little too late.

Faint, achy, and exhausted, I struggled inside and up the stairs to my room. My landlord, Mr. Blake, squinted at me from his armchair. Judging by his expression, he'd heard about what happened, but he said nothing. Not that I expected him to. The old man was made of wariness and spite. One day, I'd be able to afford something better, but considering that my meal ticket had just had his head blown off, that day wasn't going to be anytime soon.

My room had always been small, but now the whitewashed walls closed in so tightly that it was hard to breathe. I ripped off my tie and threw it as hard as I could. It fluttered onto the typewriter on my desk. Cursing myself for ruining it with ink and oil, I retrieved it and draped it on my clothes rack. It was only then that I realized it was already ruined: the bottom edge had a bloodstain from me leaning over Donnie's body.

I groaned and sank onto my bed. The world wobbled. Was this the medication or simply sadness? The line was too blurry to tell. In the ringing, spinning silence I finally cried.

Chapter Four

BY THE NEXT morning, the sedatives Martin had given me were out of my system. Not that the world seemed any less loose on its axis. I'd been around death, sure—I was the one who found my dad's body when I was fifteen—but this was different. Someone had purposefully ripped Donnie's kind soul away from the world. I felt like I was moving at half speed, bogged down by the idea that I'd never see him again.

It's not fair.

That was the only thing that was clear in my fogged mind. It was one thing for mobsters to kill each other over bootlegged gin, for sleazebags to be gutted in back alleys, for bad people to get what was coming to them. But this? Where was the justice in shooting a man just doing his job? A man who had sat with me while I struggled through enough arithmetic to graduate high school. Who had bought me the biggest dictionary and thesaurus he could find when I announced my intention to be a writer. Who had never pressed me about my seemingly non-existent romantic entanglements. Who... I ran a hand down my face. The list could go on forever, but the point was always the same: Donnie had deserved better than he'd gotten.

I needed to do something, anything. Write? No. My brain was too cluttered. Something more practical, then. Plan the funeral? *Yes, I should probably do that*. But I had no idea where to start. Burial plot? Pastor? If Donnie had ever stuck to one kind of religion, he'd never told me. Funny how all those details never quite make it into everyday living.

At the very least, I'd have to tell his family. His parents were long dead, I knew, but was there anyone else? I had a vague memory of him once mentioning a nephew in Chicago. Illinois to Connecticut was much too far to come for a funeral, but I still had an obligation to tell the man. I couldn't recall the name off the top of my head, so I decided to hunt down Donnie's address book.

Which meant I'd have to get into his room. Which meant going outside, which meant I'd need to look somewhat civilized. So I ran a brush through my hair and picked the darker of my two remaining suits off my clothes rack. It was charcoal gray wool, too warm for May, but it was as close to black as I had. I'd never gotten around to buying proper funeral attire. I made a mental note to at least borrow a mourning armband. Martin probably had one.

I dared to peek in my mirror to check how presentable I looked. The most noticeable thing about me, by far, was the bruise around my nose that had spread and darkened. *Walked into a door.* That was the excuse I'd used for similar damage done by my father. I pushed the awful memory away and examined the rest of me. My hair, an ugly off-beige and ill-behaved at the best of times, flopped into my red-rimmed eyes. Embarrassment flowed up my neck as I realized I'd looked even worse at the police station when Severo Argenti stared me right in the face. I sighed. What was done was done, and the only thing I could do was move forward.

ONCE I'D MOVED out on my own, Donnie became a boarder in the spare room in a family house, if the space could be called a room. It was more of a lean-to off the back with its own door. I'd met the owners a handful of times, but they never seemed interested, and neither Donnie nor I cared much about them either. So when I got to the building I barely recognized the landlord standing there with Detective Harlow. A couple cops walked in and out of the back door with an air of snooping disdain.

"Can I help you?" I asked.

Harlow turned to me with a frown. He was even bulkier standing. His coat, buttons straining around his gut, seemed to be held together by force of will alone. "I should be asking you that," he said. "You shouldn't be here."

He was right, I didn't have a legal right to be there, but I was annoyed now, and I never made the best of decisions while angry. "I'm Mr. Kemp's heir," I said, straightening. I hoped that sounded impressive and plausible. "Everything in there belongs to me."

Harlow laughed, sharp and deep like a big dog's bark. "As if he had anything worth writing a will over." He turned to the homeowner. "You can go. We'll find you if we need you."

The owner nodded once, then darted back into his front door. My molars ground together as I held back shouts. He was a coward and a colluder and–

An officer stepped up holding an envelope, ruining my train of thought. "Found it in the dresser, sir," he said.

Harlow snatched it out of the man's hand, then shooed him away. He opened it. I caught a glimpse of a stack of bills. "This what you're after?" he snapped, waving it in my face.

I gaped at it. There had to be at least a couple hundred in there, almost a year's salary. I would have guessed Donnie was saving it for a rainy day, but I knew for a fact that he'd begged his landlord for mercy a couple times. Why would he have done that if there had been emergency money right there? Had the cops planted it just now?

"Nothing to say, eh?"

I shook my head. "I don't know what that's from."

"I bet you don't. Well, in that case, why don't I hold on to it as evidence?"

"Evidence of what?"

"I don't know yet, but we'll find out." Harlow sneered. "Now, get going. You're not allowed to be at the scene of an investigation."

I would have dearly, dearly loved to punch him straight in the face and give him a bruised nose to match mine, but I loved not being in prison even more. I left, cursing under my breath.

I started toward Martin's place. His door was always open. If anyone wanted to talk, they could walk right in. But as I got closer, I realized I didn't want to be talked to or coddled or otherwise sympathized with. I wanted to *do* something, I just didn't know what yet. So, I passed Martin's house and kept going into the center of town.

The buildings weren't so lousy there, made of brick, concrete, and steel instead of wood, tin, and wishful thinking. A couple civic edifices had draped black bunting across their doorways, but otherwise life coasted on despite the assassination. The poor waited on the mission's breadline while the better-off got on with their shopping. Trucks puttered down the street, and the trolley clanged down the line. It was so usual, so commonplace, and I was happy to lose myself to its bustle.

While waiting at a crosswalk, I noticed Emma Carlisle and Marc Logan coming out of the police station. I'd never seen Emma in black before, or her hair pulled into so severe a bun. The only reason I recognized her at all was she was leaning against her father, and I could pick Logan out of a crowd at a hundred paces. He was at least half a foot taller than everyone else and as pale as a waterlogged corpse.

I was about to duck into an alley—they were the last people I wanted to deal with—but Emma caught sight of me.

"Mr. Dawson!" she called.

I froze, then turned, trying my damnedest not to look like I'd been trying to flee. "Mrs. Carlisle, Mr. Logan," I said. I struggled with what else I could say. "I wasn't expecting to see you today." Not great, but not untrue.

"Nor were we," said Logan. He gripped my hand a little too tightly as he stared me straight in the eye. I squirmed under the intensity of his glare. "We were called in to help give insights as to what might have happened."

So, they had been pulled in for questioning. But the police had been a little more courteous about it for them. I could guarantee no one was ransacking the Carlisle mansion and demanding to know where *their* money had come from.

"I'm so sorry about what happened last night," I said, hoping they would accept my polite condolences and go on their way.

"As are we," murmured Emma. "We understand that you and Mr. Kemp were very close."

Certainly closer than she'd been with her husband, but I kept my mouth shut and nodded.

"We would like to pay our respects to him," she continued. "Do you know what the arrangements are?"

"Uh, no, I'm afraid I don't," I answered. "I'm not even sure any arrangements can be made. I don't think there was any insurance or anything. And the police just confiscated the money he had, so..."

"Oh, that poor man! Please, let us help."

She looked to her father, and without even saying anything, he pulled a hundred-dollar bill out of his wallet and held it out to me.

"I can't take that," I protested. I wasn't about to borrow anything I couldn't pay back.

Logan shrugged and went to put it back, but Emma slipped it out of his hand. She looked up at me through long lashes. It was the sort of look I'd written about for the pulps. I didn't know that people actually did that. Odd.

"It's a gift. We insist on helping pay for the funeral," she said. "Mr. Kemp died in the line of duty. It's the least we can do." Her voice choked up. "And now that Roy is gone, money just doesn't seem as important."

That all sounded very fake, particularly the part about Carlisle's death making her think less about money; the woman had to be dancing a jig on the inside now that she was a wealthy widow. But if being the focus of her charity would keep Donnie out of a pauper's grave, so be it.

I took the bill from her hand and slid it into my coat pocket. I felt Vern's business card there. His demand burned through me like an electric current. Well, Emma and Logan were right here in front of me. It would be now or never.

"I did just want to say what an honor it was to serve your husband," I said, "and I deeply regret that I wasn't able to stop the killer. If only I'd seen something." I paused for dramatic effect. "I don't mean to upset you, Mrs. Carlisle, but... did *you* see anything? Hear anything?

I know the police are saying the shots came from the direction of the stage, but it's just... I'm sure we're both going crazy not knowing what happened."

"No. I was... I was watching him watch that *tart*," she whimpered. "If I hadn't been so jealous, I might have been looking somewhere else, and I could have stopped them, and then he might still be alive." The whimpering turned into little sobs.

Logan collected her against his side. He covered almost her entire body with his arm. "I will thank you to not upset my daughter with unpleasant questions. The police have done enough in that regard."

"I'm sorry! I didn't mean it like that..."

"No, it's all right, Alex. I may call you Alex, yes?" Emma peeled herself away from her father. "We've both had a very traumatic loss."

With fingers as white and thin as ivory chopsticks she adjusted the lapels of my jacket. It was a very intimate gesture, especially for someone whose husband had been alive the day before. I glanced at Logan, but he just watched her. Maybe that was just how the rich and powerful lived. Everything was practically theirs anyway, might as well touch it.

I took a half step back. "Well, um, did *you* see anything, Mr. Logan?"

He grunted and shook his head. "No, but I told the police this has Rutherford's slimy hands all over it. When he knows he can't win, he gets... creative."

That was the second time John Rutherford had come up. Sure, he was an obvious suspect, being Carlisle's opponent, but that seemed too simple. Even a man like Rutherford couldn't just hire an assassin and then bribe his way out of a murder charge. Right?

"I'm sure Mr. Rutherford wouldn't do such a thing," I stammered.

"You're young still," said Logan. "By the time you get to be my age, you will believe anyone capable of anything."

His words sent a shiver down my spine. I had to get out of there before things got even more uncomfortable. I cleared my throat. "Well, as long as you told the police about your suspicions... Thank you again for the money and your kind words, but if you'll excuse me, I would like to go home and get some rest."

Logan nodded once, vice-gripped my hand again, and turned away.

Emma took the same hand and cupped it between hers. "It's a pity we never got to know each other better, Alex. Perhaps we should remedy that when everything is settled." She did the eyelash thing again and, this time, added a coy look over her shoulder before following her father down the block.

It was one of the stranger encounters I'd had in my life. But one good thing that came out of it was I now had something for Vern to latch on to. John Rutherford *had* to be a better lead to chase than me.

I went to the nearest public phone and asked for the number on Vern's card. It took a little while to get through, but when I did, he was ecstatic to hear from me. He told me to meet him at a diner a few blocks from the *Westwick Journal*'s office, so I headed over. He arrived only a few minutes after me. Somehow I managed to convince him to buy me a sandwich before I would squawk. I told him what happened between bites. The dizziness I'd been fighting since the day before started to subside.

"Let me get this straight," Vern said as I chewed, "Emma Carlisle gave you money and then flirted with you? In front of her father. You're making this up."

Of all the things for him to harp on. "I'm not making it up. But that wasn't the point! Several people now are pointing the finger at Rutherford."

"Yeah, okay. Why?"

"Because he wants to be mayor. And believe me, he's rich as Croesus, so he could pay off whoever he wanted."

"Then why not just buy the election? Easier than killing a man."

"How should I know? It's not like I know the guy."

"Then maybe you should."

"No! I'm not going to go stalk someone because you're too lazy to do your own job."

I froze. The words had come out of my mouth before I could stop myself. I watched Vern for signs of anger, but he smirked.

"You got some guts, talking back like that." He leaned on his elbows. "I like it. And actually, Dawson, I like you. You play it straight. Maybe it's because you're not bright enough for guile, but honesty is honesty, and that should be rewarded. Rutherford can wait. I have a different job for you."

"Yeah, and what's this one?"

"I need someone to go chat to some people who work at the Ostia."

"Yeah, sure, and get my teeth kicked in by the mob for snooping. Which one of them owns the joint anyway?"

"Bella Ferri."

Also known as Bella Bellissima, the Queen of Sin. Well, that explained why her cousin was hanging around to blow smoke at me. It also explained a lot about the gaudy decorating. I'd never seen a picture of Bella wearing less than several pounds of jewelry. Not that she needed them. Her moniker of "most beautiful" was well deserved; she was very pretty with dark eyes, smooth skin, and thick dark hair that curled over her shoulder seductively. With a face like that, she could have had anything she wanted, and evidently she wanted to control huge chunks of the black market in booze and guns and everything in between.

And *she* was the one in charge, not her husband Dario. A lot of rumors swirled around him, some more fanciful than others. They said Ferri's hair was entirely white because he'd been so scared when Bella almost died of Spanish Influenza. Another was that he didn't speak a word of English, which was why he was only ever seen whispering into Bella's ear. The romantic in me enjoyed the story about their supposed elopement, holding a gun on a priest until he performed the rights. I intended to use that one in a book somewhere.

"I dunno, Vern," I said. "What if it was Bella who ordered a hit? Carlisle was running on a platform of cleaning up the streets."

Vern chuckled. "Don't you know it's bad business to kill your customers in your own place? Makes a mess if nothing else."

He had a point. If Bella or any other mob boss had wanted to do it, they could have done it whenever. Especially if it was supposed to be a political point. Carlisle had stood in front of crowds of people giving speeches loads of times.

"All right, tell you what." Vern leaned back. "I can get you a contact."

"If you've got a contact, why don't you just ask him?"

He gestured at himself. "For one thing, your skin color isn't going to get you thrown out of places. Second, he'll like you. Trust me. Third, you have a good reason. Me, I'm just a nosy snoop. You, you're a kid out for justice. Pity is always a good ploy. Four, I got a different lead to follow." He pulled a letter out of his jacket pocket and tossed it onto the table.

"What is it?"

I flipped it toward me and opened it. It was several pages long, written in a very neat hand. Almost too neat, like someone was trying to disguise how they normally wrote. It was addressed to Carlisle. As mayor he had received his share of threatening letters, though none of them had ever amounted to much, at least from what I'd heard.

I skimmed the contents. Starving masses. Anarchy. Communism. Fall of the oligarchy. Usually these sorts of things were rambling, but this one was almost as well written as the things I turned in for pay. Not that it wasn't heated. It ended with the trite phrase, "Or you will pay in blood." If I was going to write threatening letters, at least I'd come up with something a little more creative.

Vern grinned. "Now, that's an angle, isn't it? 'Mad Anarchist Shoots Mayor.'"

"Do you always think in headlines? Anyway, don't anarchists bomb things?"

"I guess it would depend on the anarchist."

"Where'd you even get this?" I asked.

"I have my ways."

I pushed the letter back to him. "More blackmail, you mean."

Vern crossed his arms. "For your information, this arrived at the paper today anonymously. Nothing crooked about it at all. You can ask anyone. I didn't have to do anything."

"I like that you don't even deny that you're blackmailing people."

"I do what I've got to do, same as you." He looked at his watch. "Okay, I've got to go now. But I'll get you in contact with Bellissima's guy. Call my office tomorrow before ten. I'll give you better details."

And just like that, he was out the door, leaving me with the bill.

Chapter Five

ONCE VERN LEFT, I gave up and went to Martin's. He was right, being alone wasn't good for me. Plus, the hundred-dollar bill was burning a hole in my pocket. Martin was a better person than I was, and wouldn't be tempted to use it for himself.

He stared at the bill after I dropped it on the table. "And you just took it?" he asked.

"It's not like I stole it," I protested. "They know me and Donnie are broke. Or, well, *I'm* broke. They were just being nice."

Martin frowned and tapped a finger on the table. "I'm not sure I'd call them nice. But I'll hold on to it if that's what you want." He picked the bill up like it was something disgusting and tucked it in a ceramic jar. The lid rang against the hollow insides as he closed the container. "I imagine the coroner won't release the body for some time, but have you started any of the preparations yet?"

"Uh, no. I don't even know how to start."

"No, you've never had the occasion to, have you?" He sighed as he eased himself back into his chair. "I'll take care of it."

"I can't ask you to do that."

"You're not asking, I'm offering. You have enough to think about right now."

Well, he wasn't wrong. And it wasn't like I *wanted* to do it. Some twisted part of me was convinced that if I wasn't looking at a casket, Donnie's death wasn't real.

"Thanks," I said. More kindness I didn't deserve.

Martin waved a hand like taking on funeral planning was something he did every day. "Caring for the dead is the easy part. You're the one who has to keep going."

TO MY RELIEF, no cops were waiting for me when I got home. Maybe Harlow had decided that I was telling the truth about my ignorance. I wondered what other "suspicious" things they had found at Donnie's place. What were they doing going through his stuff anyway? He hadn't been the murderer; he had just been unlucky.

Or had he? Maybe he had seen the assassin and had to be eliminated. ...Or had he known something worth killing over? He did have all that unexplainable money, after all, and he had shown up for his shift suspiciously early. Had he known something was going to happen?

What had Harlow said, that I was distracted when the murders happened? I couldn't deny that. Had that been the point? Had Bella sent a man to keep me occupied? If so, that was risky on her part. More likely, she would have sent a woman to do the job. But even if she, like Vern, had somehow gotten a hold of my police record, there was nothing to say I'd flirt with the person she put in front of me. And why even bother? I was pages into my notebook by that point, blind to the world.

I wrapped the thoughts around and around in my mind, but nothing came of them. Nothing *would* come of them without more information. I was almost glad Vern sent me after the Ostia staff. Someone was bound to have seen something, and maybe one would even be chatty enough to tell me about it. And, well, if they refused, I was no worse off than I was now.

But they didn't refuse, or at least that was what Vern said the next morning when I called him. He told me to meet the manager of the Ostia by the front entrance at four, just before the place opened. I wasn't sure why the police hadn't closed it down temporarily, if not entirely. Money had been passed under the table no doubt, but there was nothing I could do about that. Anyway, it'd be stupid to defy Vern now, especially when this would benefit me as well.

I was shocked to see Severo Argenti smoking next to the entrance when I arrived. I held back for a moment, scrutinizing the man, making sure it was him, but it definitely was. His left eye was blackened—from Harlow or another cop, I couldn't be sure—but he had the scar and the same nonchalant air about him.

When he saw me, he straightened and tugged on the bottom edge of his jacket. "I didn't think I'd see you again," he said. "To what do I owe the pleasure?"

I gaped. "*You're* the manager?"

His eyes widened as he realized I was the person he had agreed to meet. "I am. I see you were expecting someone else." He extended a hand. "I don't think I ever introduced myself. My name is—"

"Severo Argenti," I blurted. "I mean, I... The police told me."

"Ah." He retracted his un-shaken hand and let it drop to his side. "And Mr. Temple told me yours is Alexander Dawson."

I nodded and shifted my weight. I had expected awkwardness, but not quite this much.

His eyes drifted to the ground and back up. "Please, call me Sev. My friends do."

"Sure thing. And, um, Alex is fine."

Sev chuckled, and the crow's feet appeared at his eyes. "I don't think Mr. Temple knew we'd met already, if that's what you were thinking."

"Oh, no, I..." Well, now that he'd said it, it did seem very strange. What were the chances? Then again, broken clocks were right twice a day. "Maybe it's just luck?"

"Knowing Mr. Temple, I think not." Sev's smile dimmed. "Though I think you were very lucky to be at the bar with me. You have my condolences for the loss of your colleague."

I wanted to tell him that Donnie had been more than a colleague, but that would have been too much. I'd just met this man. He didn't need to hear my sob story. "Thanks," I mumbled.

Sev cleared his throat and gestured at the door. "Shall we go in?"

The scent of bleach hit me like a train. It was so strong that my eyes watered. Someone had cleaned in a hurry. Or gotten rid of evidence in a hurry. One or the other. I scanned the room. The tables had been rearranged, moved from neat rows into a random scattering. If someone had wanted to see exactly where Carlisle and Donnie had died, they'd be hard-pressed to figure it out.

Sev began leading the way in, then stopped. "Oh, wait. Here."

He stepped toward the coat check and reached over the counter. He brought up a cardboard box filled with carefully arranged hats, scarves, and a handful of jewelry. My notebook, now tied in twine, was tucked behind a pair of gloves. He pulled it out and handed it to me.

"I believe this is yours," he said. "I didn't read it, if you were worried. And I made sure no one else did."

I ran my hand along the cover, taking solace in the familiar texture. At least I hadn't lost everything. "Thanks! I thought the police had taken it or you threw it out..."

Sev shook his head. "I believe the police did flip through it, but they left it here, along with these other items." He returned the box to where he'd gotten it. "It's bad business to lose your customers' things."

I chuckled. "Good to know you have a strong service policy."

"I would hope so. I am the manager of the place, after all. I pay my taxes, unlike our friend Capone." Sev broke into his radiant smile, but he dropped it when he saw I wasn't mirroring the gesture. "It was a joke. We don't know him personally."

"No, I, uh, got it. I just... It's kind of... not what you expect, is it? Mobster making jokes and folding gloves."

He didn't frown exactly, but the crow's feet melted away. "I'm used to people making a great deal of assumptions about me. I've found that they are very rarely correct."

I blushed. Somehow, I had put my foot in my mouth astonishingly fast. For half a second, I expected him to throw me out. But his annoyance seemed to pass, and he shrugged.

"But I imagine that happens to most people, yourself included," he said as he started walking across the club floor again. "They say not to judge books by their covers, but how can you not? You can't pry open every book, now can you?"

I just nodded, not risking opening my mouth again. Sev led me between the rearranged tables, behind some curtains, and through the doors to the backstage area. It was bigger than I expected, cavernous with crisscrossing steel rafters. We wove between a crowd of stage hands and chorus girls. I followed close behind him so as not to get separated. He flowed more than walked, trailing the scent of tobacco and rosewater, and he greeted everyone with a smile and a laugh. He seemed charming, if not downright friendly.

Christ, Alex, get it together! He could kill you right now if he wanted!

But he didn't seem like he wanted to. More the opposite. How much of a threat could a washed up bodyguard be anyway? Apparently not much because I was being granted deep access without a second thought.

"Does, uh, Bella Bellissima know I'm here?" I asked.

Sev paused. The crow's feet in the corners of his golden brown eyes crinkled in concentration. "The arrangement was between Mr. Temple and myself."

So, she didn't know. That was a little worrying. What if she found out one of her soldiers—and a cousin at that— was playing games behind her back? But I didn't have time to ask him questions because he stopped at a door and knocked.

"What'dya want?" demanded a woman's voice from inside.

"It's Sev!" he shouted back. "And company!"

"Well hold on, I'm not decent."

Sev shrugged. "My apologies for the wait, Mr. Dawson. Women and theater. Both need a lot of time to prepare for a good show."

The door opened, and a brunette woman stuck her head out. After some staring, I realized she was the alto who had been singing when Carlisle and Donnie were killed. She was in the later stages of putting on make-up. This close, it looked all wrong, everything exaggerated: too pale on the face, too dark on the eyes, too bright on the lips. Her dress was the slinkiest thing I had ever seen, with a plunging front and sequins embroidered across the shoulder straps. She had a bitter frown. So much for the story I'd been composing about her as a farm girl who'd run to the city and made it big.

"What?" she snapped.

Sev bowed in mockery, the motions exaggerated. "Mr. Dawson, let me introduce the beautiful Molly Ravenna."

She grunted and rolled her eyes before stepping away from the door. She flopped onto the nearest stool and stuck a cigarette between her teeth.

With her out of the way, I could see the room. Half the space was taken up by a costume rack loaded with feathered and sparkling dresses. The other half was a long wooden table with cosmetics and accessories scattered across it. Two mirrors with lights surrounding them were mounted on the wall. The wall itself had been whitewashed, but it was peeling enough in a corner that I could tell that everything had once been painted blue. Apparently the lavish decorations of the front didn't extend to the dressing rooms.

I cleared my throat and tried not to look panicked. I had never done this before. From what I'd gathered in my experience with the police, questioning people involved a lot of angry shouting and accusations. But that seemed like the worst approach. Wouldn't shouting at people make them not want to talk to you?

"I know you're busy right now," I said, "but do you mind if I ask about what happened the night Mayor Carlisle was killed?"

"Oh, spare me," grumbled Molly. Smoke curled out of her nostrils like a dragon.

Sev's perpetual smile took on a sharp edge. "Miss Ravenna, Mr. Dawson is a guest and politely asking–"

"You shouldn't have let him in here." She sneered. "Wait until Bella finds out what you'll do just to look at a pretty face."

He put on a mask of indifference. "I don't know what you're talking about."

"Don't give me that. I saw you trying to get a piece of him that night. What's he doing, holding out until you do him a favor?"

His cheeks flushed crimson, except for the line of the scar, which stayed white.

"Hey," I growled. "I thought I was the one asking questions here."

Molly looked me dead in the eye, then shrugged. "I was singing. Bodyguard looks up, past me, somewhere on the right catwalk. He looked confused. One shot. The bodyguard falls back. And before anyone can even take a breath..." She folded her hand into the shape of a gun. "Bang. There's a bullet in the mayor's head."

"You didn't look to see what Donnie, I mean, the bodyguard was looking at?"

"I did. But the lights were in my face. I just saw someone running. Could have been anyone. The stage crew doesn't pay too much attention. They don't give them enough money to." I waited for her to say something, anything else, but she kept staring me down. After a few seconds, she stubbed out the spent cigarette.

"So, Sev," she continued. "Don't worry, I won't tell Bella you brought him in here. For a price."

Heat started building up around my neck. How dare she? Who was this woman who could treat death and blackmail so casually? I took a step further into the room, temper pushing me forward, but Sev nudged me out of the way. He sighed and pulled out his wallet. Two fives slid out from the leather into Molly's palm. She glanced at them, then stuffed them into the front of her dress. She put another cigarette into her mouth as she snapped the case closed and put it into a little clutch purse. She stood, still smirking.

"Pleasure doing business, boys," she said. She coasted out of the room swinging her hips the whole way. At the last second, she turned and tapped Sev on the behind with her purse. He flinched. She laughed and wandered off.

I thought he might shout after her or something, but he just shook his head. "My apologies. That was... inappropriate."

"You're just going to let her do that?" I hissed.

He shrugged, glancing into the mirror for a second before turning off the lights around it. Without them, the room plunged into twilight. "It's just a few dollars. Money isn't as important for me as it is for other people."

It was almost what Emma had said to me, but somehow out of his mouth it sounded more honest. Again, the question came to me: *This* man was Bella's best killer?

"What about the redheaded girl?" I asked. "The French singer. Is she around?"

Sev nodded. "Ah, Birdie, yes. She's around here somewhere..."

We took another walk through the backstage until we found the singer Carlisle had been drooling over. Unlike Molly, Birdie looked very young, maybe even younger than me. She was primping in the reflection of a glass panel of a door offset from the general bustle of the hall. A gauzy pink robe with lots of ruffles draped haphazardly off her shoulder, revealing something yellow and silky underneath.

Sev extended his hand. "Mr. Dawson, please meet our beautiful Lucille Oiseau."

"Please, call me Birdie!" she exclaimed with a heavy accent. She extended her hand like she expected me to kiss it. I didn't. Instead I awkwardly tried to turn it into a handshake. She pulled her hand back and looked scandalized. This close, I noticed her eyes were rimmed in red, though I couldn't be sure if it was from crying, lack of sleep, or some kind of narcotic.

Sev chuckled. "Birdie, Mr. Dawson would like to ask you some questions about the night of the unfortunate, er, incident."

She pouted. "Again with these questions? We already told the police we know nothing."

"I'm not with the police. I just want..." I hesitated. What *did* I want? Just to get Vern off my back? No, I wanted the truth. "I want to know what happened to my friend. The man that was killed who wasn't the mayor? His name was Donald Kemp, and he was the best man I ever knew."

"Oh, that's so sad!" cried Birdie. She wrapped her arms around me. I froze as she started patting my back. "But he is with the angels now. Nothing can hurt him."

"Uh, thanks?" I tried to slide out of her grip. What was with all the unsolicited touching lately? "He was a, uh, good man."

"Birdie, *dolce*, focus please," said Sev as he pried her off me. "Mr. Dawson is rather busy, as am I, so if you don't mind..."

She giggled and took a step back. "Okay, I'm ready."

It took me a second to regain my composure. "Did you see anything? Someone on the catwalk, maybe?"

She shook her head. "No, I have gotten up to use the powder rooms, and when I come back..." She waved a hand. "It is already happened."

Dead end. "But you must know something!" I begged. "Did you see anything unusual that night?"

Her little mouth twisted as she thought. "No. But I thought it was unusual that Mr. Kemp has not come by the day before."

What? "Why would he have come around?"

Birdie grinned and lowered her voice. "It has been for a month, he comes very late when we close and brings me to where Roy is." She giggled again. "The mayor liked me, yes?"

Well, that explained some things. But if Birdie had been carrying on an affair with Carlisle, why wasn't she more broken up? Even Emma had sniveled a little bit, and she was as cold as a block of ice. And now I had to come to terms with Donnie being a runner for an affair. What else hadn't I known about?

A disheveled man clutching some sheet music ran up. "Sorry, Mr. Argenti, sir," he panted. "I've got to borrow Birdie to go over something."

She shrugged and went with him, leaving me and Sev alone in the middle of the whirlwind of staff.

I brushed at the wrinkles all the hugging had put into my jacket. "She seems, uh..."

Sev nodded. "The war was not kind to her family, as I understand it, and it made her...peculiar."

"Peculiar is fine. I just wanna know if she's a liar. Or if she's nutty enough to shoot the mayor."

"Lying? No. As you just heard, she doesn't quite have the sense to lie, otherwise she probably would have thought one up to avoid the scandal. As for murder, I would say she is harmless." He sighed. "But you never know with these things. I try not to make assumptions."

Heat rose in my cheeks. "I'm, uh, sorry about before. I'd just... There are stories, you know?"

He smirked. "If you are interested in stories, you could have just asked me. I could tell you a few."

Had the furnace turned on suddenly? "Yeah, that would be great," I said before I could stop myself. Well, if I was already in it... "Care to go over some now?"

"If you insist." The crow's feet reappeared. "But maybe we should go somewhere more private? I know a lovely place down the road."

"Won't they miss their manager, though?"

Sev shrugged. "Working here is like herding cats. But luckily, cats tend to be able to sort themselves out when left on their own."

I didn't have anything to say to that, so I nodded. He grinned radiantly and gestured toward a back exit. "Then please, after you."

Chapter Six

GRAY, EARLY-MORNING light gave my room an almost mystical haziness as I sat on the edge of my bed. Sev brushed his hair with the aid of the tiny mirror mounted above my dresser. There was a bigger one in the shared bathroom down the hall, but he had almost been seen twice already during the short trip and didn't want to risk another. While Mr. Blake was going to throw me out at the end of the month when I couldn't make rent, I wasn't fond of the idea of getting the boot that day.

I had asked Sev about his place, but he admitted that since he wasn't married, he still lived with his mother. As bad as getting caught by my neighbors would be, getting caught by her would have been worse, so my crumbling single room it had to be.

It hadn't been my brightest idea, indulging on a whim. I could have at least stuck around the Ostia and talked to a few other people. But he was charming and handsome, and when it had come time to go home, I had been too lonely to let him leave.

"I keep waiting for you to ask me if I know anything," Sev said, looking at me through the reflection of the mirror. His forehead wrinkled as he continued brushing his hair back. The curls weren't nearly as tame as they had been the night before, but I liked them better tousled, as well as the dusting of a beard he had acquired overnight.

"Dunno what you'd know. You were with me at the back. And I figure if you did, the police would be holding you."

He smiled sadly. "Most likely. They can be... overzealous."

I nodded. We both had the bruises to prove it. It made me wonder what would happen if Bella caught wind that he'd let me go through her place.

"Why'd you agree to see me anyway?" I asked.

"I trust Mr. Temple."

"Christ, *why*?"

Sev laughed. The sound of it made little bells go off in my head that urged me to laugh with him, but I managed to keep a straight face. He smirked at my reflection. "You don't like him," he said.

"I wouldn't say I don't like Vern, just..." How to word it? "He's more interested in selling papers than being honest."

"He is. But it comes in handy sometimes."

"Like when?"

"When it keeps you safe in prison."

Right, he's a murderer.

Sev saw me blanch, and he put the brush down and turned. "I *have* killed a man," he said quietly. "That part is true."

"Just...*one* man?" Then where had the other dozen come from?

"As far as I know, yes. I'm not some kind of mad dog. There was a fight and knives got involved. He slashed at Bella. And maybe I panicked or maybe I got angry or maybe I thought I would be a hero. Next thing I know, my own knife is in between his ribs." He rubbed at his palm and looked at the floor. "I'm not proud of it. Bella tried to hush it up, but..."

It was a wild story, one I wasn't quite sure I believed. But he looked so genuinely guilty that I had to hear the rest of his explanation. "So, what? Vern made up the other murders?"

"Well, there were... disappearances at Bella's behest, but I had nothing to do with them. I just adjust the ledgers, I'm not an assassin. Your friend Mr. Temple was the one who decided to imply that they were my doing."

"But why'd you let him?"

Sev spread his arms out, emphasizing his gracile build. "Look at me. I'm not a circus strongman. I'd only been in jail a week and I'd already gotten this." He traced the line of his scar. "But if someone told you I could snap your neck as soon as look at you, then I'm more intimidating. So when Mr. Temple came to write his article, we agreed on some lies that could help both of us. They treated me a lot better after that, prisoners and guards, and Bella didn't seem to mind the rumors."

"And you were let go," I said, remembering the headlines from a few years ago. "Hung jury."

Sev nodded. "Would *you* vote to put away someone The Queen of Sin would miss? I know *I* wouldn't."

"And what did Vern get out of all this?"

"A raise, I think. They sold almost twice as many papers in the month around my trial."

I wasn't sure if that necessarily made me trust Vern, but it softened my opinion of him a bit. At least his schemes could bring some good. Of course, Sev could have made the whole damn thing up. But my gut said, like it had been saying the whole time, that he was just not a murderer. Hell, I had a hard time believing he was a mobster.

Sev's golden eyes raked over my face, an odd sort of half smile on his lips. "Well say *something*."

"Oh, I, um..." What could I say? My brain was still catching up with everything, so I said the first thing it reached. "You launder money, you said."

His brows knit together. "Yes?"

The envelope of money Harlow had confiscated from Donnie's room flashed through my mind. What if the police had been onto something? Not that it was Donnie's dishonest money, per se, but that he was holding it, waiting, trying to make it into something more reputable.

"If someone had some money," I mumbled, "not a lot, but enough. Hidden in a false drawer... How likely is it that it was dirty?"

Sev shook his head. "I couldn't tell you. Depends on the man."

I nodded. Now I felt stupid for asking. I had just wanted some confirmation that Donnie hadn't done anything wrong. Ever.

Sev sighed and came back to the bed to sit next to me. "What is this money?"

I hesitated. Should I tell him? Well, he'd been so honest with me... "The police found a couple hundred hidden in Donnie's room. It wasn't savings. If it had been, he would have used it to bail himself when he had rent trouble a few months ago."

"Ah." Sev's foot tapped for a moment while he thought about it. "Well, you didn't hear this from me, but there have been some rumors that someone was trying to fix boxing matches. More than they already are, that is."

Boxing. Pearl's dad Bert Taggart was a boxer. He might know something. In fact, he might even be involved. If I was broke, Taggart was smashed into a million pieces, so it wasn't too much of a jump to think he might be willing to take a dive. But what the hell was Donnie doing mixed up in something like that?

"Don't make faces, *caro*. You asked, and I told."

"Yeah, I know. Sorry..."

He lifted my chin with his hand. "If I'd known you were so innocent, I would've sent you home last night."

I let my lips brush against his. "But I *am* home."

There was a loud knock on the door. I jumped away from Sev so fast I nearly threw him off the bed. Had Mr. Blake had found out I'd brought a man home? I opened my mouth to ask Sev to hide, but he was already edging himself so he'd be behind the door when I opened it. He'd probably done this dozens of times. I hoped he could see the apology in my eyes.

I took a few breaths before yanking the door open, but to my surprise it was just Pearl.

"Hi, Mr. Dawson!" she chimed. "Have you seen Daisy?"

I swallowed startled curses. "What? No. Don't you have to go to school? Or something? How did you even get in here?"

"It's Sunday. And they unlock the front door at seven, and it's almost eight." She glanced around me. "Has your friend seen Daisy?"

My heart-rate kicked back up. "My friend?"

"I could hear you talking to someone." She pushed past me into the room. "Where'd he go?"

Maybe if I humored her, she'd go away. "Maybe I was talking to a ghost."

"Don't be silly. He's hiding behind the door isn't he? I can see his shadow."

I sighed. "You might as well come out, Sev. Else she might send bloodhounds after you."

Sev stepped forward. He smiled awkwardly and waved. "Hello there."

"Hi! Have you seen my cat? She's orange and black with a white tummy. Her name is Daisy."

He looked at me, then back at her. "No, I haven't."

Pearl let out an exaggerated sigh. "That cat, always running off."

I bent down so I could look her in the face. "Pearl, you can't tell anyone I had a friend over, okay?"

"Why?"

"Because Mr. Blake doesn't like it when I have people over, and I'll get into big trouble. Do you understand?"

Her eyes got even more huge, and she nodded. Undoubtedly her imagination was running over all the punishments she'd ever received. "I won't tell anybody," she whispered.

"Good girl." I patted her on the head as I stood up. "Have you asked Martin if he's seen Daisy?"

"She ran away from there," she answered as I shooed her toward the door. "Daddy wasn't up yet, so I asked Mr. Martin for breakfast. I ate an egg and when I finished, she was gone."

I launched into an internal rant against Bert Taggart and all the useless alcoholics of the world. Now, I was definitely going to see him, if only to punch him in his already much-punched face.

"Well, maybe you should go back around," I said. "Daisy's probably sitting on his porch right now."

Pearl stopped resisting my attempts to usher her out. "Maybe you're right. Sometimes she hides in the space underneath," she mumbled as she wandered out of my apartment and down the hall.

I shut the door and leaned against it in case Pearl changed her mind. "Sorry about that."

Sev laughed. "I don't mind. I rather like children. Pity I won't be having any of my own." He picked some lint off my lapel. "I should leave too. Before you get more unexpected visitors." He stepped around me and reached for the doorknob.

Suddenly I realized how desperate I was to have him stay. "Do you have to? There's a Jewish deli down the street that's open Sundays. We could pick up some sandwiches and eat in the park."

"Tempting. But I've been missing for long enough. My mother will be worried. Besides, I have to go to church and pray for my filthy soul." He went to kiss me, but glanced around the hall and instead squeezed my hand. My heart twinged with disappointment. *"Ciao, caro mio. We'll see each other soon."*

NOT LONG AFTER noon there was another knock on my door. This time, it really was my landlord. But much to my relief, it was just to tell me that I had a call. No one in the building could afford a phone on their own, but we all pitched in to pay for one mounted on the dining room wall. It was the number I used for my contact, but it almost never rang for me.

Mr. Blake settled back down to his coffee and newspaper, and I tried to keep from looking like a giddy schoolgirl as I prepared to tell Sev that a few hours was not an appropriate turn-around time.

Vern's voice crackled on the bad connection. "So, how did it go at the Ostia last night?"

I hesitated. Anything I said could be heard by my landlord and a smattering of other apartment dwellers down for Sunday luncheon. "Uh, I talked to a woman who didn't see anything. So great job on not helping me."

I could feel everyone in the room start to listen in. They all knew very well that Donnie and Carlisle were dead and that I had been there. Nothing like shocking death to sharpen the ears of eavesdroppers.

"But that's all you did, just talk to some lady? Oh, I guess so. Word is you only spent twenty minutes there before running off into the night with the manager."

I swore loud enough that Mr. Blake looked up from his paper to give me a stern look.

Vern's scraping laugh came out even more rough over the static line. "It's okay, I thought it might happen. I knew you'd take to each other. You feel better now? Burned off some of that anxious energy?"

"You did that on purpose? To get me to calm down?"

"You threw me into a wall. I think you needed to calm down."

"If this wasn't a public phone," I growled, "I would tell you exactly what I think of you and your little set-ups."

"Why? It went bad?"

My face warmed. "...No. More the opposite."

"Then you should be thanking me. Not too many people are willing to play matchmaker."

I hoped no one else could tell my face was burning. "But why would you—"

"I have a soft spot for underdogs. And contrary to popular belief, I'm not a heartless bastard, just an ambitious one. Which is why I'm here on a Sunday, looking at that letter I showed you the other day. I have a theory. Can you come down here?"

"You put me through all those hoops just now just to ask me about a letter from some crackpot?"

"Yes, because it's fun to tease you. Come take a look at it?"

I sighed, glancing around the room. Mr. Blake was still paying more attention to me than his paper, and spinster Miss O'Malley outright stared. Probably better to get out of the house before I became a target for uncomfortable questions.

"All right. I'll come by. But no tricks about it this time."

"Done. Share and share alike, as they say. Us weirdos and freaks and dregs gotta stick together. If they can kill Roy Carlisle with no consequence, then what stops them from taking down any of us?"

THE *WESTWICK JOURNAL* offices were on the corner of First and Main in a newish building that had blank-eyed, square-winged angels brandishing swords adorning the corners. Art deco at its finest or worst, I wasn't quite sure.

The building was mostly empty—not surprising on a Sunday afternoon—just some distribution guys passing the last stacks of paper to delivery boys. Upstairs the offices were even quieter. Whole rows of desks were empty, and I almost didn't see Vern until he jumped up and waved me over.

He was stuck in the corner farthest away from the door and the windows, cramped and almost hidden from the main office. His lamp had a crack running through the glass, and his typewriter was an older model with a missing x key. I considered asking him how he managed to write anything with equipment like that, but he was nothing if not ambitious. He'd have used a charcoal stick on animal hide if he had to, and would still have put out a good story.

He tossed the suspicious letter from yesterday to me. "Do you know if there's another one of those?"

"Why, what's so important about this?"

He leaned back in his chair. "You're too young to remember, but there were all sorts of weird anarchist plots during the war and just after. Crazy stuff, let me tell you. Makes these gangster-types look like a bunch of kittens. If Carlisle was getting these letters too..."

I sighed. I knew nothing about politics, and I knew even less about what went on in Carlisle's office from day to day. "I was the evening guard," I said. "The clerks would only show me something if it made them nervous, and I never saw one of these. Even if he got them, who knows what they did with them."

"Well, Mrs. Carlisle might know. She wanted you to come see her, right?" He grinned at me. "Just tease her a little until you get what you want. That's what everybody else does."

"You're sick, you know that?"

"Are you going to help me or not?"

I shuffled my feet. "I don't know. Her husband was just killed right in front of her."

"Yeah, and you got lucky last night because I called the right people. You owe me. And you know what, while you're at it, go see if Rolling Rutherford has any. If one candidate got them, maybe they both did. That could be the big break we're looking for."

I wanted to hit him square in the mouth. A couple missing teeth and he wouldn't be nearly so smug. But Donnie's memory whispered that I was better than that. Lashing out was something my father would have done, and if I had one goal in life it was to be as different from that bastard as possible.

I took a deep breath and let it out. "Fine. I'll see Mrs. Carlisle and Mr. Rutherford for you. But I want *you* to convince Bert Taggart to talk to me."

"About?"

I almost told him the reason. I needed to make sure that Donnie hadn't been in some kind of dust-up over illegal gambling. For my own sake, if not to guarantee that Carlisle's murder hadn't been some kind of ruse to throw everyone off the real reason. It was an elaborate and crazy thought, but I was a writer in my soul, and what do writers do but come up with elaborate, crazy thoughts?

"I just want to talk about some things," I said.

Vern nodded. "You learn fast. But all right. Easy enough. Come back here tomorrow afternoon, and we'll swap."

It sounded good enough to me, and we shook on it. I left quickly before he could think of anything else to force me into. So quickly that I barely heard Vern's telephone ring.

Not my business anyway.

Chapter Seven

MONDAY MORNING, I decided to grab a paper to read on my way uptown to see Mrs. Carlisle about the letters. I tossed some pennies to one of the newsies just outside the boardinghouse door, and he handed one up to me without bothering to shout the headlines. I flicked the paper open to glance at them while I waited on the corner for the trolley to come. The first article I saw was about the Minneapolis teamsters strike. Dull. It'd been going on for a while. The second was about how Carlisle's murder was still unsolved. Congratulations to the *Journal* reporters for stating the obvious. But the third nearly made me drop the paper: *Shots at Bellissima Outside Sacred Heart.*

I read through the article as fast as I could. Someone had taken a potshot at Bella Bellissima as she was coming out of church. No one was hurt, but there was now a chip in the stairs. There wasn't much beyond that. Her whole network had clammed up, and the police couldn't be bothered investigating bad things that happened to the mob.

I lit a cigarette to calm myself and almost burned my own shaking fingers in the process. Sev had probably been there with Bella. No, only maybe. He had only said he was going to church; he hadn't said which one. Sure, he was her cousin, but that didn't mean they went to church together. Right? That had to be why Vern hadn't let me know about it. If he'd thought the man he'd sent me out with had been in danger, he would have told me. Definitely. Probably. If he had felt like it.

The clanging of the trolley ripped me from my thoughts. I tossed the cigarette into the gutter and tucked the paper under my arm before boarding. I slid onto the wooden bench harder than I meant to, jolting the paper onto the floor. I cursed as I picked up the scattered sheets.

I didn't know why I cared about the gunfire at the church anyway. It wasn't like Sev was a long-term thing. He was mob, after all, and older by a longshot. How could I be anything but a toy to him? And even if I wasn't, and he was hoping for something lasting too, it couldn't work out all right like it did for other people. There was no point in wishing for the impossible.

The trolley took me up to the Carlisles' neighborhood. It was a fancy place: a couple Victorian, a couple Italianate, but mostly beaux-art homes with arches and too many detailed carvings. Even the fence that separated the Westwick River from the street was intricate, all wrought-iron flowers and vines. Altogether it was the gaudiness of the Ostia on a neighborhood scale. I could have been angry about how people lived up here when my own neighborhood was one hard gust of wind from toppling over, but I wasn't sure what could be done about it. Except possibly going the Bolshevik route. Maybe Vern was onto something with the proletariat coup angle.

The massive Carlisle home was on the plainer side considering the surroundings. White and square, it actually resembled a house rather than a castle, the most notable feature being a series of Corinthian columns across the front. Logan lived there too, rattling around by himself in a wing that was almost as large as my whole boardinghouse.

I knocked, and a maid let me in. I recognized her, but for the life of me I couldn't remember her name. I had never even bothered to learn it, figuring that Emma would dismiss her after a few months, just like all the others. The girl flitted into another room, and returned with Emma following.

"Hello Mr. Dawson! What brings you here?" she asked.

"I came around to see if you were doing all right." Not a lie, but not anything resembling the truth either. Was I getting better at this investigating thing? "Is this a bad time?"

She hovered there for a moment, uncertainty in her eyes. Then she stepped to the side with a welcoming gesture. "Mrs. Green is here, but I'm sure she wouldn't mind an additional guest to tea," she said. "And, well, you are no longer my employee."

I winced at the dig. Was it even a dig? If it was, would I have to forgive her, since she was technically in mourning? She continued regarding me with blank pleasantness for a second, then led me toward the parlor. I'd been in that house about a million times, and yet it never felt like a home to me. It was so clean, and not in the way that Martin's place was clean. Everything here was shiny and polished, new and untouched instead of worn and cared for.

The parlor was no different than the rest of the house, though there were a couple antiques that had belonged to Carlisle's mother. She had been a collector of taxidermy, and there was a cache of overstuffed birds in a china cabinet, as well as fox that was mounted with its mouth pulled into a grimace.

Sitting on a chair next to the fox, also showing distressing signs of age, was Mrs. Green. She held a teacup with crooked but delicate fingers. "What's this, Emma?" she sniffed. "Has this louse come looking for a bonus he didn't earn? Failed in his duty, didn't he."

I closed my eyes against the insult; it had hit harder than many a punch I'd taken. "Mrs. Green," I said as politely as I could through clenched teeth. "It's good to see you again."

She huffed and sipped her tea.

Emma took a seat, but didn't offer me a chair. "Oh, Elizabeth, do be kinder to my guest." She looked at me. "Though she has something of a point. What brings you around unannounced?"

I cleared my throat. "Um, this probably isn't the best time to ask, but are you keeping Mr. Carlisle's records?"

Emma's eyes narrowed. "You'll have to be more specific. I have been asked for hundreds of records by at least a dozen people. Police, insurance agents, other employees..."

"What I'm looking for are letters? Not... not private ones. They came to the office every now and then? Political stuff and threats? The *Westwick Journal* has one now, and I'm helping them see if there are any more."

"Ah. Those." She sighed. "Mr. Dawson, being a public figure isn't easy, and it certainly doesn't endear you to people. We had at least two threats a day. Luckily we kept them all in case this sort of..." She paused to regain her composure. "The police have them now."

"Oh." *Dammit, Vern. Sending me on a wild goose chase.*

"Although," Emma continued, "there was the one that came in the mail the next day, after the police had taken the others." She stood. "Wait one moment, I'll get it for you."

She hurried past me and out into the hall, leaving me with Mrs. Green. The old woman sipped her tea in silence. Then she raised her head to stare at me with eyes that age hadn't dulled at all. Sweat trickled down the back of my neck.

"So, you're really here for letters?" she asked. "Because it seems to me there are better reasons for visiting a young widow."

So that was her problem with me. "I assure you, ma'am, I have no interest in Mrs. Carlisle."

"Pity." She put the cup and saucer onto a table. "Truth be told, I never liked Roy much. He had a wandering eye, as I'm sure you noticed." She looked in the direction Emma had gone. "I can't imagine she's too broken up about losing him. I wasn't when my Henry died. A widow's money and freedom..." She brought her gaze back to me, letting her eyes track me from head to toe.

I shifted. The last thing I needed was some old lady getting ideas that I was involved in murdering a man so I could sleep with his wife. "I should, um... I should go see if Mrs. Carlisle needs any help," I mumbled.

Her puckered mouth twisted into what was probably supposed to be a wry smile. "By all means, run along then."

I flung myself out of the room, my skin crawling. Best to just get what I came for and get out. So I went for Carlisle's study, hoping to catch Emma on her way back. But I didn't run into her. I got all the way to the room and peered in. She wasn't even there. Strange. Where would they keep letters if not in the office? Actually, Logan also had an office in the building. Maybe anything that had come in after Carlisle's death was being dealt with there.

Logan's office was on the other side of the mansion, and it took me a few minutes to wind my way through the too-large house to get there. He was in—I could hear his gruff baritone echoing along the marble and hardwood before I turned the final corner.

"Don't worry, my dear," he said. "It will be all right."

I peeked around the slightly open door. Logan was at his desk, but facing Emma, who was to the side clutching a piece of paper to her chest. For once, he seemed relaxed, his icy eyes gentle. I suspected it was an expression reserved for Emma and Emma alone. But as much as I hated to interrupt the family bonding, I needed that letter. I knocked.

Emma jolted and Logan's head snapped in my direction. Whatever tenderness that had been there was doused at my intrusion.

"Oh, Mr. Dawson." Emma's shoulders relaxed. "Forgive me. I've been rather jumpy lately."

Fair enough. Her husband had been shot in front of her, after all. It could also have been the atmosphere of the room. If the parlor was uncomfortable, Logan's office was downright eerie. The walls were paneled in dark wood, and the furniture was heavy cherry lined with forest green felt. Small bronze statues of Justice and Athena brandished letter-opener-sized swords, threatening anyone who dared become complacent about where they put their elbows. And if that weren't bad enough, a dressmakers dummy loomed over everything from a shadowy corner. It wore Logan's infantry officer's uniform from the Great War. He rarely talked about his service, but I had no doubt he'd killed more than his fair share of Germans.

"I thought my daughter left you in the parlor with our other guest?" he grumbled.

I swallowed. "I didn't mean to be rude, sir, I–"

"It's all right, Mr. Dawson." Emma handed me the envelope. "Here it is. My apologies for the wait. I lost track of time speaking with my father." She stiffened, and her eyes started tearing up. "If only I was less distractible, I could have seen who…"

Where were all the waterworks coming from? She and Carlisle had been neutral toward each other at best. Then again, I hadn't anticipated how much I would miss Donnie until he was gone. I fished in my pocket for a handkerchief, stuffing the letter into its place. "Please, Mrs. Carlisle, I didn't mean to upset you."

She choked a bit, but shook her head. "No, it's fine. I'll just… If you will excuse me? It has been a very stressful time for me."

"Yes, ma'am, of course."

She scurried past me with my handkerchief pressed against her face. I remained frozen for a moment, awkward under Logan's offended scrutiny, then edged for the door myself. "Should I just see myself out or…"

"Mr. Dawson," he said as he stood, blocking out the light of the desk lamp, "I believe we had a discussion about you hounding my daughter."

My heart thudded against my ribs. Even though I knew he couldn't sack me, what with my job already forfeited and all, he was still imposing. "It was never my intention to distress Mrs. Carlisle, sir." I took a shaking breath. "I only thought she might be able to help. With solving the murders, I mean."

He watched me in silence for a few seconds, then gestured at the door. "May I escort you out, Mr. Dawson?"

It seemed like a bad idea to refuse, so I nodded. He led the way back through the corridors, his shoulders nearly brushing against the walls. I stayed a few steps behind him. He was taller than I was, well over six feet, and would have quite the reach if he decided to take a swing at me.

"I was a bodyguard myself, once," he rumbled as he plowed through the hall like a train. "For Roy's father when he ran for state senate, before I joined the Army. That was many years ago now, of course. Politics was all the rage at the time, corruption everywhere. I was nineteen and Roy was eight, just a boy." Logan turned and glared at me. "This city... It's like a magnet for the worst of everything. Every mobster from New York and Boston trundling through like we're their personal playground. Roy was supposed to have stopped it. He could have been great, Mr. Dawson. He had so much potential."

I cringed. Like I needed to be reminded that I'd been useless the night of the murders. "I'm... I'm sure he did, sir," I stammered.

Logan watched me coolly, then returned to guiding me to the front foyer. He opened the door for me without a word, and I left with a squeaked goodbye. But it was fine. I had what I needed, and Vern was going to get what he wanted, and everything was going to be smooth sailing from here on out.

Chapter Eight

VERN WASN'T IN the office when I went to drop the letter off to him, but he'd left me a message with the secretary at the front. Bert Taggart was willing to talk to me and could be found at the gymnasium by the train depot. I left straight away.

The train depot was down where I'd lived as a kid. It had been a slum then, and it was a slum now. I'd almost forgotten what the area looked like; I must have blocked it out of my mind. The overwhelming color was gray: gray concrete, gray tin roofs, even grey mud where the soot from the trains mixed with the sewage backed up in the street. Even the people were gray with poorly-dyed clothes. I shuddered as I averted my eyes from the grimy-faced children peering out glassless windows.

The gymnasium looked bad and smelled worse. Chips in the paint and holes in the walls I could forgive, but not the twisting stink of sweat, blood, and mildew. Then again, it was a windowless box of men with more muscles than brains, it wasn't going to smell like roses. I had half a mind to write down everything to use later in a story, but I didn't dare take my last handkerchief away from my nose for more than a few seconds in case I got poisoned. Why would anyone practice here when there was a new sporting arena on the other side of town? Well, I knew why. Far away from prying eyes, all sorts of malfeasance could go on without interruption.

I didn't see Taggart, and when I asked around, all I got were suspicious looks and steadfast denials. Then some skinny grunt took pity on me, or rather took the quarter I offered, and whispered that Taggart could be found in one of the equipment rooms. I went into the door he had indicated, wondering if the only thing waiting on the other side was a beating or worse. But if I didn't go in, I'd maybe never get the answers I wanted.

At first, I couldn't see much. Several of the bulbs that should have lit the room were broken or missing. Punching bags and at least half a dozen mats that had the straw sticking out were lodged against each other, creating odd angles and shadows. A thick coating of dust lined their top edges, and just under a rickety stool, a mouse or seven had made a nest out of spilled stuffing. Several dead cockroaches splayed their feet in the air, except for the one that had been crushed by someone's shoe. I battled the nausea roiling in my stomach.

I crept forward, and then the smell of alcohol hit me. The reek dragged back memories I didn't want, and I shivered despite myself. Taggart was definitely here.

"Mr. Taggart?" I ventured.

A grunt drew me forward. There was a card table behind a rack of busted up gloves. A shirtless, black-haired man sat at it with a glass and half-empty bottle in front of him. I'd once seen a picture of a Neanderthal skull, and I had always imagined Taggart's face was what one looked like with skin. His eyes were beady and bloodshot, half lost under a heavy brow ridge. He had a thick, square jaw and a nose that had been broken a couple of times. All that, coupled with arms like ham hocks, made him look like the sort of person you didn't mess with. Or at least not without extreme caution.

"I told you, if you bothered me again, I was gonna beat you until you're a smear on the pavement!" he roared without looking at me. I flinched. The action must have caught his eye because he turned. "Who're you?"

"It's Alex Dawson, your neighbor? Vern Temple said you'd be okay to talk to about..." I stopped. Maybe bringing up the fact that I thought he might be involved with fixing bouts wasn't a brilliant idea. "Your, uh, job."

Taggart mumbled a bunch of slurs and threats under his breath, then squinted at me. "What about it?"

All right, tread carefully, Alex. "Make a lot of money at it?"

"Why, you thinking of taking it up?"

He blinked. Or rather one eye closed after the other in quick succession. Anger began to edge out my anxiety. The son of a bitch was so drunk he couldn't even blink straight. I kept my face neutral, or what I hoped was neutral. Donnie had taught me to hold out as long as possible before letting things escalate to violence. It didn't always work, but I tried. And now I was trying extra hard, lest my nose get broken.

"Maybe," I answered. "Since, uh, my job fell through and all."

Taggart twitched, and his focus shifted back to his glass. "Yeah, yeah. Pity about that. But, yeah, I dunno nothing about that 'cause I was fighting that night. Made it eight rounds before Brecker got the best of me."

Only eight rounds? That meant he had to have been knocked out. But he seemed to be doing pretty well for someone who had been beaten unconscious only a few days ago. The several bruises on his face were old and faded, and his nose wasn't even as badly swollen as my own. And he had just willingly offered up the fact that he'd lost. In my experience, fighting men—hell, most men—weren't too keen about letting anyone know they could be bested. Taggart had to be on the take. But of course I couldn't let him know I knew.

"So, what's it like," I said, "being a professional boxer? You don't have a boss, do you?"

"Everybody's got a boss," Taggart grumbled into his cup.

"Right, well, who's yours?"

He straightened, and for half a second, I thought he was going to clobber me. But instead he sank in his seat again and cringed. "They'll let you know," he whispered finally.

There we go. Took long enough. "Is it one of Bella Bellissima's people?"

He nodded.

Right, so far, so expected. But what about the double-crossing Sev had insinuated was happening? Somebody had broken her fix and probably lost her a lot of money. Must have been somebody important and influential to put her on the ropes. Somebody like the mayor of Westwick?

"Is Bella the only one you have to keep tabs on?" I asked. "Or are there others?"

Taggart raised a shoulder. "Sometimes. Sometimes you get a better offer and have to take it."

Better offers, huh? "How much are we talking?"

"Enough. Sometimes you can haggle it up. And what the Queen of Sin don't know won't kill her, right?"

She might kill you though. "Who gives these better offers?"

"Dunno. Never seen him before."

That threw me for a loop. Surely, he'd know what Carlisle looked like? His picture had been in the paper at least once a week since becoming mayor. But that presupposed Taggart could actually read, and I wasn't entirely sure that he could. Plus, he barely recognized me and I lived maybe five blocks from him.

"Can you..." I hesitated over the question. "Can you describe him?"

"Mmm, stocky, black beard, brown eyes. Had a nice pocket watch, I remember."

Losing my composure, I blurted, "Donnie Kemp gave you fall money?"

"I don't know the name." Taggart peered at me. "You okay there, kid? You look like you saw a ghost."

"Um, well, he's dead," I stammered.

"Well I didn't have nothing to do with that!"

"No, I know. I didn't... Are you sure it was him?"

"Why? Was he your daddy or something?"

I just nodded. I wasn't going to explain my whole rotten history if he couldn't remember it of his own accord. He'd forget again in a few minutes anyway.

Taggart tsked. "Too bad about that. But if it makes you feel better, I don't think it was for himself."

"What do you mean?"

"I think he was playing patsy for someone. Had that awkward look about him."

I latched on to that possibility with everything I had. Donnie had only been the front to someone's graft. But who would he risk arrest or even death for? He had no family and not too many friends. It wasn't for me; I wasn't in any kind of trouble like that. That left one person he would do that for: Roy Carlisle.

But that didn't make any sense. If Carlisle had wanted to gamble, there were far more classy ways to go about it. What had he been doing that required him risking his life and reputation to fix a boxing match? The obvious answer was money, but he had loads of it. Unless he didn't...

"Do you know why?" I asked.

"I don't go around asking why," Taggart snorted. "And if you're interested in doing this professionally, you won't either."

I nodded, only half aware of what he was saying. He grunted and tossed back the rest of whatever was his glass. I caught another whiff of it. *Just like dad.* Something clicked in my head. *No more.*

I snatched the bottle of whatever the hell sort of rotgut was on the table and dropped it on the floor. Taggart yelled as it shattered, tipping out of his chair like he meant to catch what had already broken.

"Wha'd you do that for!" he cried.

"Pearl doesn't deserve a drunk for a father."

He stood, his lip curled to bare his rotting, chipped teeth. I held my ground. If it came to blows, I could take him, mostly because he was already incapacitated.

"You got no business with my girl," he snarled. "You or your slippery doctor friend."

"I do when she shows up at his place bleeding through her clothes because you caned her to an inch of her life."

"My girl, my business!" Taggart bellowed, and he took a swing at me.

I sidestepped him, and the blow missed. He roared like an enraged bull and tried to charge me. Again, I just edged to the side, and he stumbled past, falling into the shattered glass with a yelp. I figured that was the end of it and turned to go.

"Get back here, Dawson!"

I twisted just in time to see Taggart rush at me, brandishing the jagged remains of the bottle. Lucky for me getting knocked around hadn't helped his coordination, and it was almost too easy to get a grip on him and pull the broken glass away. He struggled and groaned as my elbow kept a lock around his neck.

"You can come after me all you want," I growled, "but I swear, if you lay a hand on Pearl ever again, I'll do a lot worse than just spill your drink. Understand?"

He croaked something angry, but exactly what it was was muffled by his closing airway.

A silhouette appeared in the sticky light. "What's going on in there?" someone shouted.

I released Taggart just as some bruiser rounded the corner. He gaped at us for a moment, his eyes tracking from me to the broken bottle in my hand to Taggart gasping beside me.

Shit.

I pushed past them both and ran for the door. I kept running until I was blocks away. I leaned against a wall in an alley to catch my breath. So much for smooth sailing. What had I been thinking? Harlow was already on my scent, and this would only give him more reason to hound me. But maybe Taggart wouldn't report it? Maybe he would be too ashamed of being clobbered by the likes of me that he would keep his mouth shut. Maybe he would chalk my fury up to being upset over Donnie's death. Or maybe I was soon going to be very far up a creek lacking a paddle or even a boat.

And what in God's name had Carlisle been doing mixed up with people like that? Did his wife know? Did other people know? How had Donnie gotten involved?

And stayed involved too, if those bills in his dresser were any indication. Was he being blackmailed like me? Or was there something else at play?

I straightened my clothes and wiped my face with my sleeve before venturing out into the street again. No one had chased me, and the other folks walking around didn't seem to care about the sweating, panting man in their midst, so I slipped back home before I could do anything else stupid.

Chapter Nine

I LAY ON my bed and stared at my cracked plaster ceiling, waiting for the police to come knocking. My alarm clock ticked incessantly, annoyingly, each click sending a jolt through me. I buried it under my pillow to silence it, but then I had to get up to get away from it. I paced the short distance between my door and my desk over and over in the hope that it would wear me out enough that I would fall asleep, but all it did was wind me up more.

Carlisle had been willing to pour a lot of cash into fraud and gambling, which just didn't seem logical. Not only could he lose the money, he could have lost his job, since as mayor, the whole house of cards relied on his reputation. What would make a man like Carlisle risk everything he had? Did it have something to do with Birdie and their apparent affair? Love could make a man do crazy things, after all, and if a man was also hiding something from his wife, things could go very bad, very fast.

But whatever the reasoning behind it, Carlisle had tried to undermine an already rigged system, which meant he had probably annoyed some shadowy people. Bella Bellissima, for instance, might not have found his meddling tolerable.

Something clattered outside and I rushed to the window, sure it was the cops. But there was nothing out of the ordinary, just some kids kicking a can down the dusty street in the twilight. They formed a little huddle trying to get it away from the chipped stoop.

Chipped like Sacred Heart's stairs.

Bella had been shot at too. Maybe it was a coincidence, but they were so similar and so close in time that it seemed unlikely. But who would go after both Bella and Carlisle? Was this about racketeering? Bella had chased out all the other gangs years ago, but that didn't mean someone new hadn't shown up wanting a piece of the action.

I let the curtain drop and resumed my laps. Bella had to know something. She had eyes and ears everywhere. If only I could talk to her. Maybe Sev could persuade her to meet me?

No. That would be just the kind of manipulation I had gotten angry at Vern for. But I wasn't using Sev, really. It was more like a favor. People did favors for their lovers, right? And it wasn't like I wanted him just for this. And what was the worst he could do? Say no? Say no and storm out? That put me in the exact same place I had been Saturday morning, which in the grand scheme of things hadn't been all that long ago. What was a little more heartbreak anyway?

Decision made, I grabbed my hat and headed for the Ostia.

BY THE TIME I got there, it was almost nine, and dinner-hour was in full swing. The backstage was a zoo, the impression emphasized by the peacock-feather bustles on some of the dancers. How was I supposed to find Sev in such chaos? I drifted for a few minutes, but I got turned around somewhere between the identical costumes and shuffling set pieces. No wonder the killer had gotten in and out without anyone seeing.

I got the attention of a stagehand. "The manager, Mr. Argenti, is he here?" I yelled over the ruckus.

He looked me up and down for a moment, squinting with suspicion. Then he shouted something in Italian at another man, this one rushing by with a stack of sheet music. I recognized him as the one who had hustled Birdie off the other night. He scanned me, then shouted back in the same dialect.

The stagehand nodded. "Come," he grunted.

He stomped his way through the crowd until we reached a door marked *Private*. He opened it without another word, and as soon as he had ushered me inside, he shut it again.

The office I found myself in followed the general style of club portion of the building. The walls had heavy wood panels and metal accents, but without the dizzying rococo carvings and unnecessary sparkling crystals. Ledgers were piled on the desk, though I suspected they weren't the real ones.

I took a seat in one of the leather-upholstered armchairs set facing the desk. My heart raced, and I craved a cigarette. But I still hadn't been able to justify spending some of my dwindling funds on buying my own. So instead I took to chewing on my nails.

Sev slipped in a few minutes later. He smirked as he shut the door behind him. He wore a well-tailored pinstriped suit that accented his slim figure. "Missed me already, *caro mio*?"

"Yeah, I did, actually." I stood, hoping he didn't notice me rubbing the saliva off my hands onto my pants. "I got a little nervous after what happened to you after you left yesterday."

He laughed and waved a hand like being shot at didn't matter, then pulled out his silver cigarette case. He selected one and offered it to me. I took it gratefully. My lighter made sad clicking sounds as I struggled with my slimy, shaking hand. He laughed and lit it before getting his own.

"If I'd known you were this adorable when flustered, I'd have played harder to get."

"I came to ask you something," I said before my mouth could close in protest. *Don't mess this up, Alex.*

His smile took on a confused edge. "All right?"

I was all set to beg to see Bella, but the words caught in my throat. Instead, the other question rattling around in my mind fell out. "I'm not just some boy you're fucking, right?"

Sev's eyes widened. Smoke poured out of his nose as he shook his head. "Why would you ask such a thing?"

"A guy's gotta know, right?" I tried smiling, but I could feel that the muscles in my jaw were too tight for it to look natural.

"Well I won't lie to you, I went in thinking yes, but now..." He ran a hand over his hair. "Now, I don't know."

I had expected the yes part—he was a lot older and a gangster and we'd met less than a week ago. It would have been a shock if I was anything *but* just a toy to him—but I hadn't expected it to feel like I'd been run through with a hot poker.

"What do you mean, you don't know?"

Sev chewed on his lip for a moment. "I like you, I do. You're very...sweet and well-meaning, and I haven't run into a lot of that in recent years, but I can't exactly bring you home to mother, can I?"

No, of course he couldn't, but what kind of excuse was that? My face burned with embarrassment and anger. At least the hurt gave me the push I needed to ask what I had intended to.

I took a quick drag on my cigarette before I said, "I need to talk to Bella."

He blinked at the sudden change of topic. "What do you want Bella for?"

"She gets shot at a few days after Roy Carlisle gets killed? A little suspicious, don't you think? If they're connected, I want to find out how."

Sev swore in Italian, smoke billowing out of his mouth, and looked away. "Is that all you're interested in me for? Information?"

Great job, Alex. You made it worse. But it was done now, and I was going to run with it. "Look," I said, "if we're gonna use each other, we should be honest about it, right?"

He faced me again, and his golden eyes bored into mine. I had no idea what he was thinking. It was possible I'd ruined any chance I'd had with him, but I *needed* to see Bella. She was my only link to what had happened that night at the Ostia. If I didn't talk to her, I might never know who killed Donnie.

Then Sev slid an arm around my waist and pulled me close. The sweet smell of rosewater mingled with the tobacco on his breath. "You know what, I don't care," he said, his smirk returning to his face. "Ask me again."

There they were again, the bells. But I had to shut them out, at least until I got what I'd come for. I meant to step away, but his hand drifted downward from the small of my back. I let him do it, amazed how fast my willpower could crumble.

"Can you get me in to see Bella?" I croaked, forcing my focus away from the heat flooding through me.

"For you, *caro*, I will try. She's not always open to suggestions."

"Good enough, I guess."

I leaned down and let the smoke in my mouth mingle with his. After a few seconds, I forgot all about Bella. Hell, I forgot about the whole damn mess. But what was an hour or two? It wasn't like the dead were going anywhere anyway.

I WOULD HAVE to wait to see Bella, of course. Only gods and angels managed miracles that quickly, and nobody I knew was either by a stretch. Sev said the earliest he could manage would be for some time on Tuesday night, which wasn't too bad, considering the circumstances. I could wait twenty-four hours, especially since I had to check in with Vern to tell him what I suspected about the racketeering.

When I got to the *Journal* offices on Tuesday morning, he was typing frantically. I went to greet him, but he held his hand up. I stood there until he'd done a few more lines. The typewriter made a mechanical ripping sound as he pulled the paper out, sending the familiar, bitter smell of ink into the air. He shouted to an office boy, who raced up and snatched it from his hand before charging for the door.

At last, Vern deigned to look at me, his mouth carved into a frown. "What d'ya need, Dawson? As you can see, I'm kind of busy." He *did* look busy. He also looked exhausted. Dark circles, sagging posture, the works. I wondered what had happened, but knew better than to ask.

"I talked to Taggart." I took a breath and scanned around for eavesdroppers. But Vern had been ignored in the corner for years, and no one bothered paying us any attention. Still, I leaned in to whisper it just in case. "Roy Carlisle was involved in racketeering."

Vern's eyebrows rose. "Well, well, the golden boy was tarnished after all. Got any other dirt?"

I mulled it over. "He was having an affair with that singer–"

"He *what*?" He jumped up, scattering papers off his desk. A few people glanced over. "When'd you find that out?"

"Saturday night, when I went to the Ostia. She's one of the singers."

"And you're just getting around to telling me this now?"

"I got distracted," I protested. "And not just by...my own things. You were making all those demands about getting the other letters. What even happened to those?"

Vern snorted. "I'm still waiting on Rutherford's. And I don't appreciate you trying to get tricky with me, Dawson."

"How am I tricking you?"

"You brought me some fake bullshit before."

I shook my head. "I don't understand."

"Oh, you don't understand?" He ripped the anarchist letters out of a drawer and laid them side by side. "Look at them. This is the one that was dropped off here. The other is what you brought back from Mrs. Carlisle."

At first, I couldn't make out what he was talking about. They were just letters, practiced black cursive on creamy paper. But as I stared, I realized he was right. The words on the right sprawled wider, and the capital A's had an extra bit of line across the middle that then flowed into the next letter. It was just enough of a difference for me to realize that they were different people.

Shocked, I grabbed both and skimmed through them. Yes, they both yammered on about unfair capitalist ventures and whatever other things people were saying these days, but the tones rang differently. The one in my left felt impassioned and desperate and sad. It was even somewhat smudgy, as if a frantic hand laid out the emotional plea. The right was more precise, like it was checking boxes on its way to winning an argument.

"Shit," I mumbled. I had not expected this. I looked at Vern. "Honest, I didn't know there were two of these crackpots."

He huffed and took them back. "You know the only reason I believe you is I don't think you're smart enough to lie."

I ignored the insult. "Does it make any difference if it's one guy or two?"

The anger melted off his face. "No, I guess it doesn't." He slumped into his chair and rubbed at his eyes.

"You all right?" I asked. "You look like hell, and you're snapping at me for doing what you wanted."

He sat there staring at me for a few seconds, his brows knit in concentration. He stood. "Come with me."

I followed him as he snaked his way through the office, down the stairs, and out onto the street. There weren't too many people around at this hour of the morning, and it was quieter outside than inside. Vern sat on the front steps with a groan. I sat next to him. It probably looked strange, two grown men on a stoop like lazy kids, but I was willing to look a little odd to hear Vern out. It was disconcerting to see him anything but assertive.

He stared at the traffic. "A couple weeks ago, they told us they're going to have to let some people go come the summer. They haven't decided who yet, but..." He turned to me and gestured at his face. "Easy choice, right? But I figured if I could be the one who helped them sell the most, maybe they'll go colorblind when the time comes."

I wanted to tell him that his fears were unfounded, but that just wasn't true. And getting a new job probably wouldn't be in the cards either, not at his age. At a loss for what to say, I said, "Well, I'm sure you could get by with your savings."

He shook his head. "I don't have any."

As far as I knew, Vern didn't have a wife and kids, and I was fairly sure he didn't have a lavish lifestyle. I knew they paid him less than his colleagues, but surely not *that* much less? So where had all the money gone?

He must have seen my confusion because he reached into a pocket of his jacket. He drew out an old, crumpled daguerreotype. "I didn't want everyone seeing this," he said as he handed it to me.

The image was a Victorian family portrait: parents, a girl about thirteen, a boy about ten, and a baby on the boy's lap. Something was off about the baby—his head was misshapen and none of his facial features seemed proportional, and he listed to the side despite being held firmly in place. My eyes wandered back to the child holding the handicapped one. He had glasses and a short, square figure. I was looking at Vern as a kid.

"That is my sister Nora and my brother George."

I passed the photo back. I felt like I'd been let in on something very private. "And you take care of them?"

He nodded. "Well, Nora takes care of herself, but she only makes a maid's salary. Part time too. She can't live with them, she's gotta be with George most of the time."

And here I had been thinking that Vern was just aggressively ambitious for the sake of it. "I'm sorry," I mumbled.

He laughed once, bitterly. "Bet you are." He stretched his legs out and used the bannister to haul himself back up. "Damn back. Anyway, thanks for that stuff about Carlisle's little side projects. It might not make people happy, but it'll cause a splash. Now get going. I bet you haven't written a word all week."

I nodded. He was right. I needed to sell a story soon or I'd be in even worse straits than I already was. "Well, just... If you need something..."

Vern laughed again and shooed me away. "I'll blackmail you for it."

Chapter Ten

AFTER THE LITTLE show with Vern, I decided that it would be best to check right away if Rutherford had his own threatening letters. While I was there, I could feel out if he had any guilt over what happened to Carlisle. Not that I thought he would tell me if he had been responsible, but sometimes people slipped and spilled more than they meant to.

Rutherford's office was located on the top floor of the tallest building in town, a fifteen-story stepped block of glass and cement with a strange gazebo-like clock tower on the top. A particular quirk of Westwick, the buildings got uglier as the owner got richer. The hideous clock struck one a few seconds after I stepped into the elevator. The single loud bong echoed loudly enough along the shaft to make me flinch. The operator threw a concerned look over his shoulder at me as he closed the grate. I pretended I hadn't seen him do it.

The office itself was shabbier than I'd anticipated for a man who made his money by owning buildings. Sunlight streamed through dust onto old carpets and ponderous furniture. The floorboards bowed under the weight of filled bookshelves and steel filing cabinets. A jowly man in an oil painting glared down at me from his place in a curlicued frame.

The young but tight-bunned secretary told me Rutherford had just left for lunch and wouldn't be back for some time. Just my luck. I chose to sit in one of the provided armchairs and wait rather than come back and risk missing him again. I had my notebook; I could while away the time. I dropped the story I had based on Molly and started a new one about a golden-eyed count and the plain stable boy who caught his eye. Purely for my own amusement, of course.

The clock bell clanged twice more before the door opened and Rutherford limped in. Corpulent, wrinkled, and mustachioed, he looked very much like an old-fashioned robber baron. We'd met each other a number of times as I shadowed Carlisle at political functions and state dinners, but he walked right past me without stopping, his cane thudding with every step.

"Cancel that dinner with Johnson tonight, Ethel," he said to the secretary as he headed for his office door. "Carlisle's family is having some memorial service for him and I can't see my way out of it without looking like I don't care that the poor bastard is dead—"

The secretary cleared her throat and tilted her chin in my direction. Rutherford froze, then turned slowly. His eyes narrowed; then he paled, and I knew he'd made the connection about where he'd seen me before.

I stood and tucked my notebook away. "Mr. Rutherford, sir. It's nice to see you again."

"Right, yes!" he exclaimed with false cheer as he took a hesitant step toward me, his hand extended. "Good to see you too. Carlisle's man, er, Davidson?"

"Dawson, sir. Alex Dawson."

"Yes, yes, of course. I'm very sorry about what happened to Roy. Have you been waiting long?"

"Over two hours."

Sweat beaded on his forehead. "Well, we don't want you waiting another moment, then! Ethel, hold all my calls until after Mr. Dawson leaves."

The secretary nodded her understanding as Rutherford led me into his office. He closed the door after me and stumped to the other side of his enormous mahogany desk. A huge bookcase took up the whole wall behind it, and I could have drooled with jealousy.

"Please have a seat, Mr. Dawson," said Rutherford. "What can I help you with?"

The new leather seat squeaked under me. Martin and Logan's accusing voices floated in the back of my mind, but it would be far too bold to outright ask if he was up to no good. Besides, I wasn't a cop. I couldn't ask questions like that without getting into trouble. I might even end up arrested myself. So I tucked my suspicions away for the time being, and aimed for what I came for.

"This may sound strange," I said, hoping my voice wouldn't betray the lie I was brewing, "but I'm helping the police look into something. Mr. Carlisle had some threatening letters sent to him, of a, uh, political nature, and they were wondering if you also had them. Seeing that you're the other candidate and all."

Rutherford nodded. "Yes, several over the last few weeks. They can have 'em. Ethel's got them all out front. I told the police when I started getting them that it was going to lead to no good, and look what happened! Poor Roy, dead!"

Just the act of saying those few sentences reddened his face and made his cheeks puff out. Perspiration still glistened on his face, and he reached for a handkerchief. Was he really that out of shape or was there something else making him so flustered? Like guilt perhaps?

"Sir?" I said. "Are you feeling all right?"

He waved at me with one hand and rummaged in a drawer with the other. "Oh, don't mind me. I just get all worked up by these damn Reds. Don't know what it means to work for what you've got." He placed a bottle filled with pills on the desk. "Forgive me, it's three-thirty, yes?"

I checked my watch. "Yes, sir. Thirty-five, actually."

"Fine." He shook a pill out of the bottle into his hand and tossed it into his mouth. "Can't be too careful. Medicine is a dangerous thing. Take my advice: don't get old."

"I'll do my best, sir."

"Ha! I like a man with a good sense of humor. We could use a man like you on the campaign. Not as a bodyguard, of course, you understand, but I can find somewhere to put you if you're interested. Charming young people always entice others to the polls."

"Are you... Are you offering me a job?"

"Depends. Are you interested?"

"Uh, depends on what I'd be doing."

"Little of this, little of that. Nothing you couldn't handle."

While the promise of a new job was nice, the hairs on the back of my neck were standing up. I'd had enough hard knocks in life to know that if something was too good to be true, it was fake right down to its core. Whatever he wanted me to do, I didn't want to be doing it.

"Thank you, sir," I said, "but I think I'm going to work on creative pursuits for now."

Rutherford leaned back in his chair. "Ah, yes, I believe Roy mentioned you were trying to be a writer. Well, good luck to you, my boy. That's a tough area. Real tough." He watched my face, searching for something, then shrugged. "But I respect a good man who knows what he wants out of life. If only we had more of them, this world wouldn't be such a terrible place, eh? Now, was there anything else you wanted besides those letters?"

I shifted in my chair. "No, sir."

"Right, then." He extended a hand toward the exit. "Have a nice day. Oh, and my condolences on the loss of your employer."

I took the cue and left, disgust creeping across my spine. Martin and Logan had been right: Rutherford was about as clean as a sewer rat with fleas. But I doubted unwitnessed, vague conversations and my personal discomfort were going to convince anybody that he was slimy enough to have his political opponent assassinated. I needed hard proof.

Ethel was banging away on her typewriter as I stepped through the door. "Hello again!" she chimed.

"Hello. Mr. Rutherford said I could see the threatening letters that came in a few weeks ago? I'm bringing them to the police."

She looked at me, her youthful face lost under her thick glasses, and nodded once. "One moment, please."

She stood and smoothed out her skirt before stepping across the room to a row of filing cabinets. She pulled out a drawer near the very bottom and started rummaging, her back to me. I glanced across the top of her desk. Typewriter, pens, blotter, eraser, scissors, ink. Of course. Who would keep incriminating things in plain sight? With one eye on the secretary, I nudged open a drawer. It scraped in its slot. The secretary straightened and looked right at me.

"Is everything okay?" she asked.

I faked a cough. "Dusty in here," I mumbled.

She cocked her head but then returned to her task.

I chanced peering into the gap I'd created. Notebooks. Bingo. But how was I going to grab one with Ethel and her sensitive ears not twenty feet away? Maybe I could talk her into leaving the room somehow?

Entirely too soon, she closed her own drawer and stood. With my heart hammering, I looked at the desk again. If I left the drawer open, would she notice? Could I close it without having to put my acting skills to the test with more coughing?

That was it. Not one cough, but a whole fit.

She approached with a small stack of envelopes. "Here you are, sir. Is there anything else I can help you with?"

I took them from her and placed them in my pocket. "No, thank you, this is great. I'll just be–"

I dredged up the raspiest rattle I could. Then another and another. Already my throat hurt from forcing it, but it was all or nothing now. I hunched forward as I continued, hoping that might sell it a little better.

On the edge of my vision, Ethel wrung her hands. "Oh dear, oh dear, are you all right? Would you like some water?"

I nodded. I must have looked pretty bad, because she bolted from the room.

As soon as the door closed, I took a deep breath to stretch my confused lungs. I peeked at the entrance to Rutherford's office. It was thick oak. It was doubtful he'd heard, and even more doubtful that he'd come to investigate. Perfect.

The first thing I went for was the drawer I'd already opened. They were notebooks all right, but full of actual notes in a spindly shorthand I could only presume was

Ethel's. I dropped them back into the desk and slammed the drawer, frustrated.

Where would I keep evidence of corruption? It had to be well-hidden, but easy to access in case it needed to be destroyed quickly. My eyes lit on the shelving. So many books. One could be exactly what I was looking for, hiding in plain sight.

I ruled out several shelves at a glance. The topmost and bottommost had dust all over them. No one had been near them in months, maybe even years. The middle two had been used much more recently. I scanned the areas that had a little more polish to them. Many of the books that had been taken and replaced were tomes of tax law, economics, and history according to their spines. I pulled on them one by one, checking that they were what they claimed to be.

A book on President Buchanan proved to be what I was looking for. It was much lighter than I expected, and when I opened it, it was hollowed out, and a notebook slightly smaller than my hand was inside. I rolled it up and jammed it inside my jacket, then shoved its empty case back into the shelf.

A shadow moved across the glass of the door. I only had a few seconds to take up my place by the desk again before Ethel crept in with a glass half-full of water.

"Thanks," I fake-wheezed as she handed it to me.

"Is there anything else I could do for you?"

I shook my head as I drained the glass. "I'm fine. Asthma acting up is all." I gestured at the city sprawling beneath the window. "I get nervous around heights."

"Oh, yes. It used to make me jumpy too, being up so high!" She smiled and took the glass back. "You get used to it though. Have a nice day, sir."

I returned her cheery wave before hustling back out to the elevator. The operator gave me the eye again, but I ignored him. I had what I'd come for. Blood rushed in my ears. I hadn't bluffed so hard since I was a teenager. What would Donnie have said if he knew I'd lied straight to some poor girl's face? But he would have understood. Sometimes bad things had to happen in the name of good.

I SWEPT INTO the Ostia with the contraband ledger tucked inside my jacket and went straight for Sev's office, ducking around the perpetual shuffle of staff. For all my underage troublemaking, I'd never stolen before, and the nerves made me into a woodpecker on the door.

"*Entra*," he called.

The word had barely reached my ears before I barged through. I slammed it behind me and flipped the lock. Sev stared at me from behind his desk, his brow furrowed in confusion and concern. He smashed his cigarette into the almost-full ashtray in front of him.

"Please tell me you're running in to call off the meeting with Bella," he said.

"What? No." I leaned against the wall to catch my breath. "Why would I call it off?"

"Wishful thinking on my part. You are in trouble, then?" His eyes scanned over me. "And don't deny it. I know what it looks like."

Not quite how I wanted to ask another favor of him, but since he was already on-target, I pulled out the ledger. "I took it from a hiding place in Rolling Rutherford's office." I checked the lock one more time before walking over to Sev's desk. "Marc Logan says Rutherford is crooked. Can you prove it?" I set the ledger down in front of him.

"You want *me* to tell you?"

"Well, you'd know better than I would, right?"

Sev closed his eyes and muttered something in Italian as he ran a hand over his hair. "Fine, fine. It'll give me something to do before we see Bella."

My mind switched directions. "She agreed?" I exclaimed. "That's great! When? Where? Are we–" I stopped when I realized Sev didn't share my excitement. In fact, he was scowling. "What's wrong? You've been cagey since I walked in here."

He drummed his fingers on the desk before reaching for his cigarette case. "Let's say I'm not one of her favorite cousins."

"Well, she must at least kind of like you, right? Otherwise you wouldn't be working for her."

Sev's head snapped up. "She tolerates me because I have a skill she needs. And I did not get a choice about whether I wanted to use it or not."

I swallowed. Somehow, I had treaded into dark water. But I wasn't about to give up on my chance to find out what happened to Donnie just because Sev had some problems his family. Hell, who *didn't* have problems with their family?

I crept over to his side of the desk and placed a hand on his shoulder. "You don't have to come, you know. I'm an adult. I can have a conversation with someone without getting myself killed."

"No, it's better if I'm there. Strength in numbers, yes?"

That seemed like an odd thing to say, but I nodded. Best not to end up in an argument. "Where are we meeting her?" I asked.

He slid a piece of paper over to me. An address was scrawled across it in pencil. "Al's Diner on Pine. Tonight."

The location was familiar, a few blocks from my boardinghouse. It was quiet and cheap, but the coffee was only decent if you held your nose while drinking. I hadn't pegged the place as somewhere the mob might stage negotiations, but then again, it seemed like I had never known anything, not even things right in front of my face. It made sense, though, when I thought about it. Empires couldn't run on swank establishments alone.

"The meeting is for ten," Sev said, a barely perceptible tremor in his voice. "I can meet you outside your building at quarter 'til."

Christ, he's really terrified of her, isn't he? "Yeah, quarter 'til is fine."

We both hovered there until he grabbed the ledger and flipped it open. "These are a lot of favors I'm doing for you, *caro*. How are you ever going to thank me?"

He raised his head and grinned mischievously, and all my apprehension melted away. It would have been so easy to get carried away again, but I wanted to know how far Rutherford's corruption went as soon as possible. Besides, I had to take another trip to Vern's office before I lost the letters.

"Tomorrow, I promise," I said as I let my fingers find his. "Once everything's settled down."

He smiled and squeezed my hand, then let it go. "I'll hold you to that. Now, go." He leaned back in the chair and brought the ledger into his lap. "I have work to do."

Chapter Eleven

VERN WOULDN'T LOOK me in the eye when I brought Rutherford's letters to him, and he barely spoke except for a grunted thanks. He kept watching me, though, like he expected me to bring up his family again. He didn't need to worry. I knew when I'd been told things in confidence, and Vern wasn't the kind of guy to talk out his feelings. When I left, though, he smiled—genuinely this time, not a predatory grimace—and I got the sense that I'd just proven my worth to a man who trusted no one.

But there was no time for warm and fuzzy feelings. I was about to meet the Queen of Sin, and I had to at least pretend I was worth talking to. It was almost nine thirty by the time I managed to clean myself up and brush out my clothes. I went downstairs to wait for Sev. He arrived at a quarter 'til exactly.

"Punctual," I said as I glanced at my watch.

"It doesn't do to keep Bella waiting."

He started straight for Pine, and I had to jog to keep up with his purposeful steps. His nervous energy crept under my skin and made me jumpy. "Did you look at Rutherford's numbers?" I asked. He nodded. "And?"

"He's siphoning money from construction bids into his own development company. Did you honestly think he wasn't after you found that book hidden away?"

"Well, you know, I had to prove it. I'll have Vern dig into it, and he'll be happy, and the cops'll *have* to look into it once it's all in the papers. I bet Rutherford got—" I tripped on a broken piece of sidewalk in my attempt to keep up with Sev's relentless march, and it derailed my train of thought. "Slow down, will you?" I said. "It's not like we're going to be late."

"Good. She does not like latecomers."

"Seriously." I had to grab his shoulder to make him stop. "Quit acting like she's going to shoot me on sight."

He stared at me a second, then pulled his hat down a little lower over his eyes and started walking again. "I would like to remind you that this is a dangerous business. There are no second chances, and there's very rarely mercy. You do not get a free pass just because you are unfamiliar with it."

That shut me up quick. It was one thing to hear rumors, but entirely another to see someone behave like their life was really on the line. For the rest of the walk, I followed Sev in silence, dodging the beaming streetlamps.

The diner was dark when we got there, maybe for the sake of mystery or maybe to save on the electric bill. It *was* after-hours after all. The building itself was long and low with a curved roof. A polished wood counter with soda levers behind it and stools in front ran the length, and booths lined the opposite wall. The one all the way in the back had a rip that had been repaired badly and would leak horsehair if someone bigger than a child sat in it. The floor was made of big white tiles that turned gray under the tables where it was hard to mop.

Someone had dragged a high-backed chair from somewhere and put it in the middle of the aisle where Bella sat in it with the air of someone too good to be here. The enormous mink stole wrapped around her shoulders dwarfed her and yet let her jewelry be seen—and she had a *lot* of jewelry. There must have been pounds of it on her neck alone. There was a looped string of pearls and at least two pendants on chains. Gaudy rings glistened on both her hands. Bracelets dangled on her wrists, and gold earrings did the same in her ears. I suspected she might rattle if she moved.

Dario Ferri, his white hair almost glowing in the shadows, stood behind her. High cheekbones and a small downturned mouth gave him a look of pride and contempt. He held himself stiffly as he watched me with narrow eyes. I wondered if he always looked so suspicious, or if it was my special treat.

Bella and Ferri had three guards. One blocked the door to the kitchen. He had a wolfish look, hungry and calculating. I didn't see any weapon on him, but that didn't mean he didn't have one. Two other guards lounged on stools near the entrance. The larger one was big enough to bend even a guy like me in half. The wiry one had nonchalant air about him. As I stood there he casually pulled out a flip knife and started paring his nails with it. If he had wanted to intimidate me, he did a great job.

I glanced at Sev, but he kept his head lowered. I wanted him look at me with his beautiful golden eyes and tell me all his warnings had been a joke. How had we even gotten this far? What had he told her to get her to agree to meet me?

Bella held her hand out to me like Birdie had at the Ostia. I had a brief moment of wondering if the French woman learned it from her or the other way around. This time, I let my lips graze the back of her hand instead of trying to force it into a handshake. I straightened, paranoia about the wiry man's knife coursing through me.

When I raised my head, Bella smiled indulgently at me. Her face was moon-pale in the dark. "*Piacere.* It's good to see some men have manners."

I backed away from her so I could keep an eye on all the players in the room. "I wouldn't want to insult you."

She nodded. "Wise." She threw a look at Sev. "Severo here insisted I speak to you. And who am I to deny such a simple request from family?"

Ferri rolled his eyes and grumbled something in Italian, contempt twisting his features. Bella answered him, giggling and patting his arm. He snorted, but some of his sour look melted away, like just hearing her voice was enough to chase out whatever upsetting thoughts he had. If they were any two other people, it might have been adorable, but since they were the most powerful mob boss in the city and her husband, the scene was disturbing. One moment, they could be laughing and in love, the next plotting someone's death.

She turned back to me, flashing a wicked smile. "Do you know what he said? He said the only reason we're talking to you is because my cousin wants to fuck you. And I told him that he already has."

My cheeks burned. Sev kept his eyes on the grimy floor. Had he told? Had Molly? Were we just that obvious?

Bella seemed amused by my embarrassment. "Anyway, you must be quite something if my darling cousin was willing to go to such lengths for you. He didn't say what you wanted, but I imagine it's money. I hear you're out of a job." She smirked again.

I swallowed the instinct telling me to get out of there before she stopped thinking I was some kind of dancing monkey provided for her amusement. "Miss Bellissima," I began. "I mean, Mrs. Ferri, uh—"

Bella flicked an impatient hand. "Signora is fine."

"Signora." I cleared my throat. "Do you know who shot at you on Sunday?"

Her eyebrows raised in surprise. "No. Do you?"

"No, ma'am, but I... I think it might be the same person who killed Roy Carlisle and Donald Kemp."

Ferri squinted at me. "*Chi é* Donald Kemp?" Donnie's name sounded so strange in his accent.

"He was the other man killed at the Ostia with Mayor Carlisle," I answered.

Ferri and Bella conferred between themselves for a minute. I looked to Sev, hoping he could give me a hint about what was being said. He only smiled weakly.

Bella turned her attention back to me. "Why do you think they are connected?"

"Well, they're similar, right? Distance shot. Public place. And you do own the Ostia."

"Hmm." She drummed her jeweled fingers on the arm of the chair. "You are smarter than the police, it seems. They think we are responsible for Mr. Carlisle's messy end. Which isn't to say I hadn't thought about it. But he was dull and ineffective, and in the end, he was wrapped around my finger just like all the others."

I wasn't quite sure what that meant, but at least she was playing nice with me. Of course, she could have been lying. I wondered if she knew about Carlisle trying to undermine her racketeering. If she did, would she be so confident that she had the upper hand?

"Then who would want to kill you both?" I asked.

Ferri shook his head. "*Nessun–*"

The sound of shattering glass reached me before the fragments did. Sev threw himself to the floor, dragging me with him. Bella yelped, and Ferri jumped in front of her.

He reached inside his jacket, but as he pulled out a revolver there was another gunshot. He fell backward into Bella's lap, pulling her down, red appearing in the center of his shirt. Another shot and the big guard collapsed at his post near the front door, his head shattered into smithereens.

Like Carlisle's.

I scrambled to my feet and rushed to the broken window. I stared out, but it was pointless. Everything past the circle of light from the streetlamp was pitch black. The shooter could be anywhere in the shadows. There had been three distinct shots, so not a tommy-gun. A rifle? A shotgun?

"Alex, get down!" Sev cried.

I turned back. He was struggling to prop up Ferri, who was unconscious and bleeding. The two remaining guards had their hands full keeping Bella on the floor. She screamed and bawled, clawing at their arms as she tried to get to her husband.

"Get down before they shoot you too!" Sev snapped.

I dropped to the ground again and took a shaky breath. My ears rang, but beyond that there was silence. The shooting had stopped. Actually, it had stopped after the big guard had fallen. I had been standing in the window for a good ten seconds and nothing had happened to me.

The wiry guard hissed something in Italian, and Sev answered him as Bella redoubled her shrieking. He looked to me. "We can't go to hospitals. They'll arrest us," he explained. "Is there a doctor we can go to near here?" He dropped his voice. "Or a priest?" Bella yelled something at him, and he cringed. "Preferably the doctor?"

Doctor? I hadn't been to a doctor in years. But I did know a doctor of sorts: Martin. While bullet in the chest was a bit more than food poisoning or a broken arm, it was the only thing I could think of.

"My neighbor," I said. "Lives a couple blocks from here."

There was some discussion, then Sev nodded. He released Ferri's limp body into the hands of the two guards and hauled Bella to her feet. She broke away from him and lunged at me.

"It was a trap!" she cried as she beat her fists against me. "You tricked us!"

I twisted away from her, letting her blows hit my shoulder and arm. "I didn't, I swear!"

"Bella don't!" Sev yanked her away from me.

She kept screaming, switching in and out of English, as Sev held her hands back. Even though he was a good half foot taller than her, I thought she still might manage to win their scuffle. One of the guards called out to her. It must have been something along the lines of not having time for this, because she stopped struggling. It didn't shut her up though. She kept spitting curses as we shuffled and stumbled out the door, leaving the corpse of the big guard on the floor.

Chapter Twelve

THE WARM NIGHT was quiet aside from Bella's screeching, her loud sobs echoing against the crumbling concrete.

"Shut up! Do you want the cops on us?" I growled as I peeked around a wall.

While I wasn't so concerned about the police, there was a decent chance an idiot neighbor might try to calm the commotion with a baseball bat or tire iron. But the stars were in our favor and no one confronted our odd little parade.

As soon as I saw the fence around Martin's yard I shouted his name. That was safe, at least. It wasn't the first time people had come looking for him in the middle of the night over some real or imagined emergency. He opened the door just as we got through the gate. Warm yellow light poured out, making him into a bold silhouette.

"Good lord, who—"

"Don't ask questions," I said as I took the porch stairs two at a time.

Pearl peeked around the doorframe. I skidded to a stop, and Sev stumbled right into me. What was she doing out at this hour? The guards dragging Ferri's body shoved us all out of the way and stormed right through the door. I followed.

Pearl's cat Daisy jumped off the kitchen table and hissed as the guards laid Ferri on it, knocking the vase of wilting irises in the process. The shattered remains crunched under my shoes.

"What happened?" Martin asked. He was already back inside, rolling up his sleeves.

"Shot," I squeaked.

I hadn't expected my voice to be so strained. I also hadn't expected my hands to shake so badly, so I balled them into fists at my side and hoped no one would notice. Nausea boiled in my stomach. Every time I looked at Ferri, I saw Donnie bleeding out on the Ostia's floor.

"Move!" Martin shouted as he shouldered past me.

I flinched. I'd never heard him raise his voice before. But then, I'd never seen him in a true emergency before. His posture straightened, and his eyes took on a fierce intensity.

He gestured at the wiry guard. "You. Get that bottle of bleach in the corner. And towels. Alex, get my bag from the den. And for the love of God, someone get that crying woman out of here."

I had almost forgotten about Bella. She was weeping and wailing just inside the door, clawing at her jewelry and mumbling in Italian. Sev, who had been holding her back, steered her outside at Martin's word.

"Alex!"

I jumped. "What?"

Martin bared his teeth at me, his already-bloodied hands working to undo Ferri's tie. "My bag."

"Right! Um, where—"

"My den. Sometime today!"

I stumbled out of the kitchen into the hall. I'd never been in Martin's den before, and frankly the definition of the word was stretched by the surroundings. It may have been a closet at one point, but Martin had somehow shoved a small desk inside. A single lamp showed a lot of fresh ink-stains on the papers and the blotter underneath, like an inkwell had tipped over. Had our screaming interrupted him? The snoop in me got the better of the situation, and I moved closer to the desk to see.

I froze when I saw the rifle propped in the corner, concealed by shadows. I hadn't seen it from the door. Ferri had been shot with a rifle most likely, and if Martin had rushed in to hide it, he could have knocked over some ink—

"Alex!"

Martin's desperate call snapped me out of my suspicions. I scrabbled around, looking for the bag. Lucky for me, it was sitting on the floor next to the door. I rushed into the kitchen with it.

The smell of bleach hit me like a punch, making my eyes water until I could barely see Ferri on the table. His tie, shirt, and jacket had been dumped on the floor revealing his bare chest. There was less blood than I expected, but every pulse leached away more from its owner.

The screen door rattled, and I flinched at the sound. But it was just Sev coming in without Bella. His face was so pale I might have thought he was the one bleeding out. It did nothing to calm my nerves.

Martin yanked his bag out of my hands with a curse. His hands were wet. It occurred to me that he had already washed up. Clean hands meant live patients. How much good it would do when the operating theater was a kitchen in a crumbling house was up for debate, but at least he was trying to keep things to the letter.

My thoughts slowed down. I was too hot. Words hit me, but they passed right through. I felt dizzy, but I wanted to help. I reached for something, some bottle. My hands were shaking so much I knocked it off the table, and it shattered like the vase had. The bitter tinge of alcohol joined the smell of blood and bleach burning my nose and eyes.

"Get out!" Martin bellowed. I didn't need telling twice.

I bolted back to the porch and pulled the wooden door closed behind me, cutting off some, but not all, of the horrible stench of the kitchen. Compared to its stuffiness, the night air was crisp and wonderful. I loosened my tie so I could drink it in. I looked over at the bench on the porch. Bella was sitting there, her stole halfway off her shoulders. Makeup streaked all down her face, and her hair was fraying from its curls. She toyed with one of her necklaces in her lap. She had tugged so hard on it that the chain had snapped.

She glanced up at me. Her eyes reflected coal black in the weak porch light, as dark and malevolent as thunderclouds. "Was it a trap?" she snarled. "Did you trick me?"

I had thought I was terrified before, but it was nothing compared to seeing the look on Bella's face. I held out my empty hands. "I swear it wasn't a trap. It was your place; how would I trap it?"

"Bribes. Threats. Lord knows what you and Severo cooked up!"

I was surprised she assumed I had that kind of guile. "What would I bribe them with? I can barely afford rent. I don't have any connections or skills. I don't even own a gun. How could I threaten anyone?"

She snorted. But after a moment, her gaze dropped to the ground. "You're pathetic."

I couldn't argue with that, but at least she didn't see me as a threat to be eliminated. I fished around my pockets for cigarettes I didn't have, and surprisingly found one. It was one of Sev's I had bummed off him yesterday. Had that only been yesterday? Had Donnie really died less than a week ago?

"Who would want both you and Mayor Carlisle dead?" I asked as I flicked at my lighter. If anything, this continuing nightmare confirmed my suspicions about the connection.

She shook her head. "I could write you a book of names of people who might want to hurt me or Dario, but as for Mr. Carlisle... I didn't care enough to even find out."

Something rustled on the near side of the fence. Panic swelled inside my chest. But it was only Pearl who appeared in the glow of the porch light, cradling Daisy in her arms as always.

"Pearl!" I gasped. "Where'd you come from?"

She put the cat down on the ground. It proceeded to lick itself. "Everybody running around scared Daisy. I had to chase her all the way through the neighborhood."

She came closer, and I saw red marks on her neck like she'd been grabbed. Every bit of the last half hour melted away. "Did your dad do that to you?"

She paused, then picked at the collar of her dress, her expression a mask of indifference. "He was mad I got my shoes muddy."

My hands balled into fists. *That bastard. Next time I see him, I'm gonna–*

"*Gattina*, come here," Bella beckoned.

Indifferent to the fact that quite possibly the most powerful woman in the state had just called her, Pearl skipped up the stairs to the porch. She stared at Bella.

"You're pretty," she said. "Like a princess!"

"Thank you. My name is Bella. What is yours?"

"Pearl." She glanced at the porch door. "Who's that man on the table?"

"Don't be rude," I scolded as I tossed the end of my disintegrating cigarette to the ground and crushed it with my shoe. Such a normal action. It was simple things like that that convinced me I was still alive and hadn't somehow died and gone to hell.

"It's all right, Mr. Dawson," Bella answered. "We had a daughter of our own once." She returned her attention to Pearl. "He's my husband, and I am very frightened that he will die."

Pearl nodded, then wandered off to the window boxes of herbs dangling off the porch rail. Trust a child to not understand the gravity of the situation. "Well, don't worry because Doctor Martin will fix him. He can fix almost anybody."

"Is that so?"

"Mmhm." Pearl plucked a chamomile flower out of the box and scampered back to Bella. "Here! I'm sorry about what happened."

"*Grazie,*" said Bella as she took it from her hand. She patted the space on the seat next to her and Pearl slid into it. "Do you want a pretty thing?" She tied the split chain in her hands into a knot, then slipped the whole thing over Pearl's head. I realized for the first time the pendant was a silver locket. Bella glanced at me. "It was a gift from him when we were first courting and we were poor. But now we have money, and he can buy me another."

Pearl opened the locket. I couldn't see the pictures well, but I could tell both sides were filled. "Who are they?" she asked.

"That is my husband when he was much younger. And that is our daughter Giulia on her fifth birthday."

"Your husband's hair is white now."

"Yes. It started losing the color when she died, many years ago."

Bella raised her head to look at me again, and I averted my eyes. I didn't want to be part of her stroll down memory lane. But apparently she had tired of her own nostalgia because she reached forward and shut the locket. Pearl flinched at the sudden movement.

"I'm sorry, *gattina*. I didn't mean to frighten you." She brushed a strand of Pearl's hair back into place. "Where do you go when your father hurts you?"

"Here sometimes," she answered. "Sometimes I just walk."

Bella nodded. "I see."

Sev came out just then, closing the door behind him. His face was lined and pallid. No good news ever came with a face like that. He knelt in front of Bella and took her hands in his. I didn't know the words he said to her, but I could feel the pain of them, the sadness. Even if I hadn't, I would have known when Bella started to wail. The flower tumbled off her lap.

No, no, no this can't be happening! With Ferri dead, Bella was going to turn on me and Sev. And I still wasn't any closer to finding out who was committing these murders.

Pearl crept over to me. "Is he dead?"

"Yeah," I mumbled, my throat closing. "I'm afraid he is."

"Can I see?"

"What? No! Why—"

Before I could stop her, she bolted through the door. I chased her. Little girls and dead gangsters were not on my short list of things that went well together.

The wiry guard was closing Ferri's staring eyes. Martin hunched, gasping, gripping the top rung of one of the kitchen chairs. His re-washed hands dripped soapy water onto the floor. While he had probably seen death on a regular basis, but having someone die in your kitchen was a bit more intimate than might be expected. Pearl ran up to him and hugged him around the waist.

It took him a second to register what was happening. He looked down at her like he'd never seen her before. And then it clicked. He crouched down, leaving damp handprints on the chair.

"Who let you in here? Go home."

She lurched away, aghast. "But you said I could stay when—"

"I said go home!" His voice ripped through the quiet like a peal of thunder.

Pearl's face screwed up, and she started bawling. Martin blinked at her. Remorse flooded over his face. He raised a hand to comfort her but stopped before he touched her. As he pulled it back, I could see it shake. Without another word he got up and walked out of the room with a distant look in his eyes.

"All right, time to go," I said as I lifted Pearl up and held her in my arms. She might be able to outrun me, but she couldn't break out. "Christ, you're heavy. He didn't mean it, you know. He's just very tired. We're all tired, okay?" As much as I regretted to think it, she'd be safer with Taggart for the night. "Let's go see your dad."

She squirmed and tried to push me off. When that didn't work, she kicked me in the thigh repeatedly, aiming for as much damage as possible.

Not keen to be doubled over in pain from a hit to the groin, I let her down. "All right, all right! We won't see your dad."

She huffed and sat in a chair with her arms crossed, seemingly oblivious to the dead man right in front of her.

Sev walked in, leading Bella by the hand. She was trying her best to keep a straight face, but tears kept pouring down. She saw the body and turned her head away like not seeing it might make it not true. Then her eyes lit on me. She hissed what I presumed was an Italian swear and spat at my feet.

Sev's eyes grew huge. "Bella!"

She ignored him and started yelling in Italian at the other two men. Her words must have been orders because they snapped to attention. The wiry one went into the hallway, and Bella stomped after him. The wolfish guard grabbed a rag from the counter and began scrubbing the blood smears on the floor.

"Sev," I whimpered.

"She's just upset right now, saying things she doesn't mean," he assured me as his hands smoothed the wrinkles of my jacket. The words were nice, but his expression was the hollow one of a man staring at his own noose. I couldn't blame him. Bella could do whatever she damn well wanted, and right now, she probably wanted us both tortured to death.

"Sev, she's gonna—"

"Shh. *Será bene, caro mio.*" He smiled. It lacked its usual sparkle.

Bella swept back into the room. "The girl," she said.

I blinked. "What?"

She ignored me and looked at Pearl. "You cannot stay here tonight, *gattina*. Would you like to come with me? I will show you many more beautiful things."

I took a step forward. "Wait just a second! You can't—"

The wolfish guard stopped cleaning the floor and stood, putting a hand in his pocket and drawing out a handgun. Of course Bella had brought insurance with her. But what on earth did she want with a kid like Pearl? Did she just want a hostage?

Pearl didn't see or maybe didn't understand what she was looking at because she broke into a smile. "Do you live in a castle?"

"No, but it is very large and very fancy." Bella held out her hand, and Pearl jumped up to take it.

I knew pleading wasn't going to do any good. Best case, they ignored me. Worst case, my body would be added to the count. Maybe Sev's too. Bella strolled past me, leading Pearl along like she was her own daughter. The wiry guard stalked out of the living room. What had he been doing? Was Martin all right? I tried to peek, but I couldn't see without turning my face away from the gun.

Just before she got to the door, Bella turned and pointed at Sev. "You're coming with me too."

He swallowed, and his eyes darted from her to me and back again. "Can—"

"Do not make me drag you," she snapped.

He hesitated a moment, then brought my face down and kissed me. I almost pulled back, but what did it matter that everyone saw now? We were both as good as dead. Might as well enjoy what was going to be my last few minutes.

"Everything will be fine, *caro*," he whispered as he let go, tears melting into his false smile.

I nodded, but only to play along.

"Now!" Bella snapped.

Sev broke away and scurried to her side. She stared at me a moment, then walked out with Pearl and Sev in tow. The guards took up Ferri's body and followed her.

I stood there for a few seconds, my breath coming in shallow pants. I wasn't dead, that was something at least. I could account for everyone except—

Martin.

I ran into the living room, sure that he had been killed. But he was sitting in an armchair staring at nothing. His troubled eyes were even redder now, with bags under them. He'd been crying. Aside from that, he didn't look too bad.

"Are you all right?" I asked.

He looked at me but didn't see. "Yes?"

Well, that's better than no.

I hauled him to his feet. He swayed for a moment, and I had to drape his arm around me in a reversal of how it'd been when Donnie was killed. Martin tottered like a broken wind-up toy, stilted and not likely to last much longer.

I'm sorry, I'm sorry, I'm sorry.

It was a relief to leave him on his bed. He curled up and closed his eyes, not even bothering to take off his shoes. I didn't know what else to do, so I just shut the door to the bedroom.

I leaned against it, nauseated and weak, then slumped down until I was all but sprawled on the floor. I stared at the front door, half expecting someone to burst through. Bella's people, maybe the police. Sev. Pearl. Anyone, just to drive away the morbid stillness. But no one came. It was just me with the knowledge that it had all gone wrong, and that it was my fault.

Chapter Thirteen

SOMETHING CRASHED, STARTLING me awake. I jumped to my feet, a hundred unpleasant thoughts running through my head. Martin's hallway blurred around me. I leaned against the wall to brace for the deathblow I was still sure was coming.

But nothing happened. More clanking came from the direction of the kitchen, but much softer this time, and a small voice saying, "Oh, drat!"

"Pearl?"

I stumbled into the kitchen. Sure enough, there was Pearl using a chair to climb up and root through the cabinets. Several pans had fallen onto the floor. She had a small iron percolator in her hands, trying to fit the pieces together.

"I'm making coffee," she announced.

My mouth fell open. How had she gotten back here? Had last night been some kind of weird dream? But no, blood still stained the table, and pieces of the broken vase and iris stems littered the floor.

"Who's there?" shouted Martin from somewhere behind me.

"Alex and Pearl," I answered.

He appeared in the door to the hallway a few seconds later, bedraggled and lost-looking, with hair falling into his face. He held the rifle but kept it aimed at the floor.

"What are you two *doing*?" he demanded.

"Making coffee," Pearl repeated with a roll of her eyes, like Martin and I were the ones being unreasonable.

He sputtered for a moment, then groaned as his knees buckled. The rifle thudded to the ground. Luckily, I was close enough to catch him before he dropped too far. I dragged him to one of the kitchen chairs, and he collapsed into it like a house made of straw.

"Hey Pearl, can you come here a second?" I called. She climbed back off the counter and came to me. Her eyes lit as I produced a quarter and pressed it into her hand. "Go down to the diner on Pi–" I stopped. Best not send her where someone shot at us. The place was going to be crawling with police anyway. "Go to the deli on the corner and ask the girl behind the counter for a paper cup of coffee. If she makes a fuss about it, tell her that Dr. Martin had to deal with an emergency in the middle of the night. Okay? You can keep the change."

She nodded enthusiastically, no doubt already plotting what she could do with fifteen cents all to herself. "Okay, Mr. Dawson!" she said as she skipped out the door. "Back soon."

"And be careful; it's going to be hot!" I shouted after her just as the screen door slammed back. I doubted she heard me, but she was smart enough to know to slow down while holding hot liquids. I was desperate to know how she had gotten away from Bella, but at the moment, I just needed her out of the picture while I figured everything else out.

"You didn't need to do that," mumbled Martin.

"No, I definitely did," I answered as I slid into the chair across from him. I tilted my head until I heard my neck crack. Sleeping sitting up was not ideal.

"Don't take this the wrong way, but you look terrible," he said.

"Yeah, well, go look in a mirror. You'll see what terrible looks like." I stifled a yawn. "You didn't eat yesterday, did you? Or the day before?"

He flushed, a dusting of red on his hollow cheeks. "How could you tell?"

"Most people don't almost faint when confronted with a six-year-old making a mess." I glanced at the door. "I should have sent her with a dollar and told her to get a sandwich too."

"Do you have a dollar?"

I rummaged in a pocket. "I've got some lint, some string, and a paperclip. If we find a nice-quality stick, we can try fishing in a puddle."

Martin almost smiled, but his dour look soon reappeared. "Alex, what the hell happened last night?"

I knew it would come to that eventually. Nobody could put on a brave face after all that mayhem, not even Martin. I tried to be as neutral about it as I could, which was difficult because I was still shaken up myself. "There was an emergency. You know how it is."

Martin straightened, anger flashing in his bloodshot eyes. "You brought Dario Ferri in here to die on my table," he hissed. "I didn't even know that's who it was until that woman was screaming in my face, swearing up and down that if I say anything I'm going to end up in an unmarked grave somewhere."

"Would you have refused to let us in if we'd told you who it was beforehand?"

He scowled. "No, probably not. But, good Lord, Alex! Bella Bellissima? What were you doing with them?"

"I thought she might know something about Donnie's murder."

He gaped at me. "I don't... I don't even know where to begin! Do you have a death wish? Because there's a nice tall bridge over the river, and you can leave the rest of us out of it."

"Hey, I didn't know someone was going to shoot up the place!" I shouted.

That outburst took all the strength I had left out of me, and all the thoughts I was trying to keep at bay poured in to replace it. Martin was in trouble now, possibly Pearl. Definitely me and Sev. I had known it before, but the fear was just catching up to me. I folded my arms on the table and put my head down. Not much of a hiding place, but it was the best I had at the moment.

"I'm sorry," I murmured. "I just want to know what happened to Donnie."

Martin sighed. I couldn't tell if it was frustrated or just tired. "People make mistakes," he said coolly. "But I want you to stay far away from them from now on."

I raised my head. "I can't."

I would have gladly never had anything to do with Bella ever again, but I couldn't just abandon Sev. Especially not after that. He'd risked a lot to get that meeting, and now that it had all gone south he was in serious danger of losing his life. For me. I had to figure out a way to fix it.

Martin stared at me, incredulous. "You're stupid, then; you know that?" His face softened. "But you're not stupid, are you? You're hiding something."

What could I say? That I'd had some wild thoughts about him being the one to shoot at us? That I was sleeping with the cousin of the most dangerous woman in town? That I'd almost choked Taggart to death? "I don't know what you're talking about."

"Alex." He reached across the table to me. "Whatever kind of trouble you're in, you can trust me."

Trust him? Could I really? I swallowed before answering. "Why do you have a rifle?"

His brows came together. Probably thought I was just avoiding his question with one of my own. "Protection," he answered. "Bella wasn't the first person to threaten me because I'm not a miracle worker. But I forgot about the damn thing until this morning. It's not even loaded. I'm not even sure it still works."

The first part was plausible, but the part about forgetting not so much. It had been leaning against the den wall bold as anything. "Where'd you get it?"

"Army issued."

I frowned. "I didn't know you were in the Great War."

He laughed uneasily. "Yes. Same battalion as Marc Logan, actually, so you can ask him if you want proof. I was a private and he was...oh, I don't remember, some sort of officer. It's not a period of my life I'm fond of. All that senseless death. But it's what inspired me to become a doctor."

I hesitated over my next question. "And why'd they make you stop being a doctor?"

"I thought we were going to talk about you?"

"You first. Why'd the hospital sack you? Must have been bad if they were willing to give up a bright young surgeon."

"I knew you'd ask one day." Martin sighed and stared at the ceiling for a moment before looking me in the eye. "I stood up for my principles, that was all. No one died. My license wasn't stripped. Nothing happened besides the arrest–"

"Arrest?"

The door banged open. I jumped up, but it was just Pearl, her hands full with a paper bag and a sloshing coffee cup. I giggled at my own skittishness. What would I have done if it was one of Bella's people anyway?

"Sorry, I spilled some," said Pearl as she deposited the half-empty cup in front of Martin. She also handed him the paper bag. I peered inside. Three apples. Presumably she had spent the change on those. Smart kid. Sweet, too. Taggart was worse than a fool to mistreat her. "Now, everyone can have breakfast," she said with a grin.

"Did Bella not feed you?" I asked.

She made a face. "She tried to make me eat oatmeal. Blech!"

"Bella?" Martin looked at me. "I thought you brought Pearl home?"

"No, I went home with the princess lady!" Pearl exclaimed. "She brought me to her house and she made me take a bath. But the water was hot and the towel was soft! Then she let me borrow a nightgown that was so long most of it was on the floor. And she had a whole separate bedroom for guests that I slept in. In the morning, she came in with a bowl of oatmeal, but I hate oatmeal, so I wouldn't eat it. And then I think she was getting mad, but then she said that she had to do something else, and I should go before you and Mr. Dawson got too worried about me. Then I came here to make you coffee." She beamed.

Martin's mouth opened, then closed as he shook his head. "I don't want to know. As long as everyone is safe..." He looked at me. "*Is* everyone safe?"

"Yeah," I assured him. "You tried to help, right? And look, Pearl's fine." I smiled, hoping he'd buy it. "We're all fine."

"You never did say why you thought it was a bright idea to go poking around the mob for information."

Damn. Almost made it. "You think the police were going to stroll up to Bella Belissima and say, 'excuse us, but did you happen to order the mayor assassinated?'"

"And you thought doing it yourself was more appropriate?"

"What's assassinated mean?" piped Pearl.

"It means killing a politician," I answered. "But they didn't have anything to do with it. At least that's what they said. But someone shot at us before they said anything else."

"Well, then *who* shot at you?" demanded Martin.

"No idea."

He paled like he was going to be sick. "This is insane..."

"It's fine," I said. If I kept pretending hard enough, maybe it *would* be fine. I stood. "And to prove it, I'm going to go home so you can eat and get some rest." *So I can make sure anyone after me stays away from you.*

Martin stood too and took a step like he meant to stop me, but he was still unsteady on his feet. We both knew he was in no condition to chase after me. Hell, he wasn't even capable of scolding me. His shoulders drooped. "All right, Alex. Do what you want. Just...try to stay safe. I don't want to see you on this table any time soon."

Chapter Fourteen

MY LANDLORD GAPED at me from the armchair in the public parlor after I walked in the door. I couldn't say I blamed him. I knew I looked awful with my clothes and hair all rumpled, but I didn't see just how awful until I stripped everything off. There were bleach marks on my shirt and bloodstains on the sleeve of my jacket, and even some small tears and grains of glass on the back from when the window had shattered. Even the knees of my pants were scuffed up. I left all the clothes on the floor and flopped into bed.

I woke up to someone knocking on my door. Orange light spilled through the space between my curtains. Dusk. I squinted at the tiny hands of my clock. Quarter after eight. The knocking continued, louder and more frantic. I remained still, hoping whoever was on the other side couldn't hear my heart racing.

"Alex?" begged Sev's voice. "Alex, please. Please be here."

For a split second, I thought it might be a trap. Bella knew very well I'd open the door for him. All it would take would be a gun to his head, maybe even less, to convince him to tempt me outside. If he was smart, he'd do anything she wanted.

But he sounded so distraught. People who were waiting to kill you didn't sound like that, right? I decided I'd rather die from a bullet to the head than a broken heart. I jumped up and pulled the door open.

No thug, no weapon, just Sev looking like he'd been to hell and back. His hair fell into his eyes, and his suit was wrinkled and stained the same way mine was. He gasped with joy and relief and embraced me.

"*Grazie a Dio*," he whispered into the space behind my ear. I felt tears drip onto my neck as he rambled in Italian. He tilted my head down and started kissing me.

I dragged him inside and shut the door. "I don't know what you're saying," I said as I came up for air, "but it's good to see you too. Are you okay? What happened? Where have you been?"

"With Bella. She made me stay with her. She was so angry I was afraid..." He ran his hands down my bare arms as his eyes scanned my torso. "You're not hurt? Your friend too? The girl?"

"We're fine. At least everyone was this morning."

"Good, good." He ran a hand through his hair, sending more of it out of place. "If you go now, get the next train–"

I shut him up by kissing him. The next thing I knew, we were falling into bed again. What was there left to say, anyway? I wasn't going to go anywhere without him, especially not after dragging him into this mess in the first place, and I knew he wasn't going to go anywhere without me. I could hear it in the way he whispered my name against my skin.

After we made love, he wove his fingers in and out of my hair, a smirk on his face. In the dark, his eyes were no longer gold, but that didn't stop me from getting lost in them.

"I guess happy to see me was an understatement," I murmured.

He laughed. "Subtle is not my strong point."

"Get me a cigarette?"

"Why don't you get it yourself?"

"Because if I get up, you'll have to get off me anyway. No point in both of us moving."

He chuckled and kissed me before climbing out of the bed. He shuffled through some of his clothes until he found his jacket. He tossed the cigarette case to me. I pulled one out, leaning on my elbow on the edge of the bed to light it.

He came up behind me and draped his arm over my waist and kissed my neck. "You could have been killed last night," he murmured.

"It's pretty obvious they were going for Bella." I blew the smoke through my nose and shrugged him off so I could sit up. "How'd you get away from her anyway?"

Sev stole the cigarette out of my hand. He took a drag on it and exhaled the smoke slowly before giving it back. "She let me go."

"She just let you go, huh? Sounds too easy."

He leaned against the headboard and closed his eyes, like thinking about it was painful. "It wasn't easy."

The story was simple enough. Bella took him and Pearl back to her house along with Ferri's body. She made Sev sit in the pantry under guard for hours in silence. Day came and still nothing, but he could hear people moving around the house, some even coming and going from the kitchen. He thought he heard a child's voice—Pearl's—but he was too anxious to be sure. Then the door opened again.

"It was Bella," Sev said. He paused to take a shaky breath. "I was so sure she was going to have me killed right there. But then she took another step inside and behind her was my mother."

"Wait, your mother?" I asked.

He nodded. "I was just as confused as you are. And *she* was confused. Who wouldn't be, seeing their son trussed up and thrown in a pantry like a ham? So, she asked why–"

"And Bella told her?"

"Bella told her *everything*. Everything about last night, including why I had called the favor. And she tossed in a few other things, too, just for the sake of being thorough." He swallowed the wavering in his voice and stared at the ceiling for a second before continuing. "The look on my mother's face... I almost wished Bella had shot me instead."

I pulled him close. My own mom was long gone, but I could still remember the sharpness of betrayal the moment I realized she had chosen to abandon me. I wouldn't have wished that feeling on anyone, let alone Sev. He let me hold him as he continued.

"Then Mama told me to get out because the mourning was for the family and I wasn't her son anymore." Sev smiled, probably because he couldn't think of anything else to do. "So I left and came here. And that's it. Everything's gone. No job, no home." He looked at me. "But I swear to God if Bella so much as touches you–"

"I'm fine," I assured him. "If she wanted me dead, I'd be dead. She's had hours to do it, and it's not like I've been hiding." I traced the scar on his face. "I'm sorry about your mom."

He shrugged. "We weren't on very good terms anyway. I think she knew, deep down. But I don't want to talk about it anymore."

I nodded and smashed the butt of the cigarette into the ashtray on my nightstand. "Sorry. What do you want to talk about then?"

He curled against me and we settled back down, his head on my shoulder. "I don't know. Your writing?"

"Ha! No. Not unless you want to fall asleep."

"I'm sure it's not that bad." He started playing with my hair again. "We should open a bookshop and sell only your books. Somewhere far away from Bella. Run away with me. I always wanted to see India. Or Australia. Everyone's a criminal there."

I couldn't deny the idea had appeal. Take the money Emma and Logan had given me and buy boat tickets to as far away as it would get us. Surely Bella couldn't have a reach everywhere. But then what? It always sounded so romantic and exciting, but once you got away you still had to live. And I'd feel guilty about leaving Vern and Martin and Pearl mixed up in whatever was going on. Donnie's ghost would always hover behind me, disappointed and sad.

"I'll think about it," I said.

Sev made a soft sound, already drifting off, and nestled closer. I let him stay there for a few minutes, content to just be there with him. But then, chronic overthinker that I was, my mind started running wild. That was four murders now, all done from a distance, and both locations owned by Bella. There was some connection I wasn't seeing.

Then there were all the other spider webs I'd walked into. Martin's secret arrest. The anarchist letters. Rutherford's corruption. Donnie helping Carlisle conduct an affair and fix some boxing. Were any of those related? Maybe Vern would have some ideas...

I edged out from underneath Sev, who grumbled and shifted, but thankfully didn't wake up. I didn't feel like trying to explain to him why I was leaving or that he shouldn't follow me. I pulled my last clean suit off my clothing rack and dressed in the dark. The sun was long gone, but I knew Vern would still be skulking around the *Journal* offices. With Ferri dead, there was no chance any reporter was going home early.

Chapter Fifteen

THE *WESTWICK JOURNAL* offices buzzed with dozens of voices and the rattle of typewriters. Three people nearly crashed into me as they ran sheaves between desks and out the door. The overhead lights blazed in contrast to the pitch darkness outside. Reporters kept peculiar hours as a rule, and big news like Dario Ferri being murdered would keep them going right until the printing. I wound my way through the mob to get to Vern's desk.

"Alex!" he exclaimed when he saw me. "Did you hear? Two deaths last night! Dario Ferri and John Rutherford."

I stopped in my tracks. Rutherford had died too? "Come again?"

"John Rutherford died!" he repeated. "Had a heart attack or stroke or something in the night. A maid found him collapsed next to his bed this morning. Dawson, where have you *been*? It's all anyone's been talking about all day."

"I, uh, I slept in." That seemed coincidental, for Rutherford to up and die only a few days after Carlisle. "They're sure it was a heart attack?"

"Well, he was fatter than Taft, so I wouldn't be surprised, but the coroner's got him now so they'll be able to tell us in a few days. Very sudden. Apparently he was at a memorial service for Carlisle at Holy Faith last night with the whole upper crust and everybody says he was fine when he left."

I nodded, only half listening. If Rutherford was dead, someone was bound to go through his office. Would they find the missing notebook? Would they be able to trace it to me? Could Sev get in trouble because I couldn't just leave well enough alone?

"You've got a weird look on your face, Dawson," Vern said. "You got something to share?"

What to start with? "I heard Rutherford was embezzling," I answered.

Vern snorted. "I'd be more shocked if he wasn't. Is that all you came here to say?"

Well, since he hadn't mentioned it already... "What about Ferri?"

"No idea. The police say it looks like something went down at that diner on Pine, but they're stretched thin, and no one on the street is talking. Why, do *you* know something?"

I nodded and leaned over his desk so only he could hear me. "Yeah. I was there."

Vern's eyes widened, and he jumped to his feet. "Details, man!"

"I'll tell you about it and you can be the first to break it, but I need you to do something else for me."

"Yeah, what?"

"I'll tell you in private."

Vern stared at me for a moment, then crossed his arms over his chest. "Fine. Anything else you want, Mr. Extortion?"

I allowed myself a smug smile. It was about time he learned what it felt like to be on the other side of the table. "Cigarettes. Coffee. And a sandwich would be nice. I haven't had anything to eat all day."

"Done."

He pulled his jacket off the back of his chair and his hat off his desk. Fifteen minutes later, we were at the diner we'd visited when I first brought information to him. It was packed, probably because the next-closest place still had police swarming around. I inhaled the hamburger Vern got me. I hadn't realized how hungry I was. Even as I ate it, I wondered if I should try to save some to bring back to Sev. He hadn't gotten a chance to eat either.

"So what is it you want me to do?" grumbled Vern.

Oh, right. I'd been so invested in the food that I'd forgotten I was trying to coerce him. "Two things. One, can I see those letters again?"

He groaned. "You should have asked me when we were upstairs–"

"And two..." I hated myself for doing it, but I needed to know. "I need you to find out why Martin was arrested."

Vern's scowl deepened. "That doctor guy that lives by you?"

"Yeah, he said... I asked him why the hospital fired him and he said that he'd been arrested. Don't know when. Maybe '26, '27. He said it wasn't violent."

"All right, well, the letters I can do. We'll go back to the office and get them. The police records... Maybe I can get them tomorrow. *Maybe.* Might take 'til Friday."

"Thanks."

"Yeah, yeah, you're welcome. Now, tell me about Ferri."

I told him the whole thing. How I'd gotten Sev to get Bella to talk to me. How she didn't seem to care at all about Carlisle. Then I told him about how Ferri had been shot through the window, and how he died of shock and blood-loss on Martin's kitchen table. I kept Pearl out of the story lest Vern think it was okay to descend on a little girl and badger her with questions, but part of me wondered what Bella's interest in her was. Had Pearl been some kind of collateral, insurance that I wasn't going to pull a trick? Or was she that torn up about her dead daughter and husband that she just wanted someone to coddle?

"But you've got to clean that up, Vern," I said. "I don't want Martin getting in trouble. And I don't want me in it either."

He nodded as he took a toothpick out of the case to shove in his mouth. "It can be done. Damn. And Bella blames you, I bet."

"She does, but I don't see how I could have done anything. She's the one who picked the place and the time. Someone had to have planned to kill her there. People don't just walk down the street in the middle of the night with rifles shooting in random windows!"

"Are you sure your new bedmate didn't make an arrangement with somebody else?"

For a horrified second, I thought about the possibility of Sev turning traitor. Was he frightened enough by her to want her dead? Maybe, but then why go through a whole charade with me? Anyway, he had seemed cowed, not defiant. "Why would he? She's his boss and his family."

Vern shrugged. "Boss and family? That makes plenty of reasons to want someone dead."

"By that argument, we could all be killers."

"We could be. Even you, Alex. One day you're gonna find something you're willing to kill for. Maybe it'll be money. Maybe it'll be your new sweetheart. Or maybe it'll be something high and mighty like patriotism or justice. Or maybe you'll just get sick of it all one day and do it just because you can."

"That's pretty cynical even for you."

The front door banged against the wall as some more patrons walked in, and I flinched. Was this how it was going to be now? Me jumping at every sound? But then I made a connection.

"The third guard," I said.

"What?"

"Bella and Ferri brought three guards, but only one died. And he was shot *after* Ferri. He was *aimed* at. Bella and Ferri were already on the floor. Why kill him? I bet he told the killer where Bella would be, and then they killed *him* to make sure he didn't become a problem later."

Vern's eyes lit. "Interesting. What do you know about him?"

"Just that he was as big as a house. But maybe Sev knew him."

Hopefully he did, and the guard would turn out to be a piece of shit, and then Bella could stop blaming us. Not that it would undo the revenge she'd already taken, but at least we wouldn't have to spend the rest of our lives looking over our shoulders.

"How are you gonna prove it though?" Vern asked.

I swallowed the last of my coffee and shook my head. "I don't know, but I have to try. It's either that or get the hell out of this city."

"You *could* just leave, you know. What've you got here anyway?"

"Not until I bury Donnie. And I'm not going to bury him until I get justice for him."

I couldn't read the expression on Vern's face. Admiration? Or just incredulity? He threw some change on the table to pay for the food. "Come on, let's get your letters."

We left the diner and walked back toward the newspaper office. We passed the Ostia on the way. It was bright and loud enough that music could be heard all the way on the sidewalk. Someone opened the door to enter, and I heard snippets of someone singing in French. It was like nothing had changed. But they all probably had it as a routine. I suspected Sev didn't manage so much as hang around and keep an eye on things for Bella. And if he was out of favor with Bella, there would be no point in him even showing up. The bigger problem for them was probably Ferri's absence. If I remembered anything from history classes, it was that losing royalty always made things an awful lot worse for the peasants.

"Hi, Mr. Dawson!"

I jumped at Pearl's voice behind me. She had come out of nowhere with Daisy in her arms and Bella's chain around her neck. She grinned, her huge eyes reflecting the streetlamps.

Vern stared at her but didn't address her. "What's this kid doing out this late?"

"You seen what Taggart does to her?" I muttered. "I'm surprised she ever goes back." I bent down to her height. "It's almost eleven, Pearl. Where are you going?"

"The trolley stop to go to the pretty lady's house. I was waiting for my dad at the gymnasium, and she drove up in her car and leaned out the window and said I could stay whenever I wanted."

Sure, Bella had taken a liking to her, but inviting her over seemed somewhat extreme. Then again, grief could make you do all sorts of things. At least this one was pleasant. Or I hoped it was. But I couldn't talk to Pearl about it with Vern next to me. Whatever was going on, the poor thing didn't need an interrogation from a reporter on top of it. Still, strange that she'd make the kid hike out on her own.

"I thought you were staying with Dr. Martin?"

"His house is cold and there's no food."

Well, can't blame her for that. Given the choice, I would have prefered a mansion over starving and freezing. I wondered if Sev was disappointed to move from sleeping in a house with a feather bed and porcelain sinks and everything else to a dusty brick apartment with cracking floorboards.

Vern threw his toothpick into the gutter. "Ah, just let her go. She's made it this far all right."

"Yeah, I guess. Wait, you know what? Pearl, wait one second."

I tore a blank page out of my notebook. If Pearl was going to Bella, I could get a message to her without putting Sev in more danger. I scratched out a quick letter swearing I would find out who killed Ferri and that she should look into the dead guard and how he had to have been the one to sell them out. I also threw in a line about how Martin had only wanted to help and that he was sorry he couldn't do more. I figured if Bella had enough pity to let Pearl stay with her, she'd have enough pity to leave at least Martin alone. Killing for spite would be bad business.

I folded the paper and pressed it into Pearl's hand. "Give this to Bella, okay?" I whispered.

"Okay." She pocketed it and skipped on her way without saying goodbye. Her cheerful manner made me feel better, at least. She wouldn't hurry toward somewhere she didn't want to be. Maybe Bella *was* doing a better job mothering her than Taggart. Though honestly a moldy carrot probably could have done that.

When we got back to the *Journal*, Vern retrieved the letters from his desk drawer for me to look at while he typed up the story about Ferri. Something had been nagging me about them, but I couldn't place it. I lined the three of them up with Rutherford's in the middle. It matched the raving one that had turned up at the *Journal* the day after Carlisle was killed. Was there some meaning in that? Maybe if I saw them in a different context something would jump out at me.

"Can I take these with me?" I asked.

Vern peered over his typewriter at me. "Hell no! I thought you just wanted to look. But tell you what, come back tomorrow. After this little trip with Ferri is over, I'm going to start looking into anarchist organizations." He grinned "It'll be fun, just like old times when Sacco and Vanzetti were big news."

"Yes, just what this town needs, more anarchy," I mumbled as I dropped the letters back on the desk.

I didn't know why I agreed so quickly except that getting Vern to budge off the Ferri murder would take more energy than I had. Too much activity on too little sleep and too little food was taking its toll. By the time I had walked halfway back to my boardinghouse, I was exhausted, my feet dragging with every step. Even if Vern had let me take the letters, I wouldn't have looked at them. And anyway, there was a bigger problem waiting for me when I got there.

Chapter Sixteen

HARLOW STOOD ON the threshold of my apartment with a nasty smile on his face. "Ah, just the person we were looking for!" he bellowed as I mounted the last step into the hallway.

I kept my mouth closed. Was this Bella's doing? Had Taggart finally called them about the assault? Or did Harlow want to ruin what was left of my life just because he could? I tried to get a glimpse of my room, but Harlow was in the way, and all I got were flashes of blue as two officers ransacked the place.

Where's Sev?

"You know the great thing about people who live in apartments?" Harlow continued. "I don't need a warrant. All I have to do is tell the landlord their tenant is up to no good and then," he snapped his fingers, "the door opens like magic."

"What are you doing here?" I asked.

"Looking for something. But never you mind. *You* need to stay away while we search." He pushed my shoulder and chuckled.

I wanted to hit him, but that was probably what he wanted. Assault on a police officer? That was years behind bars. And the right words to the wrong inmate, and I might not make it out alive. So I breathed like Donnie had taught me and went back outside.

I stood on the stoop and pulled out a cigarette, trying to look casual about this latest turn of events despite my heart beating out of my chest. Where was Sev? As I stepped down to start searching the neighborhood, a pebble clattered onto the sidewalk in front of me. I looked to where it had come from. Sev waved to me from an alley concealed from the glow of the streetlamp. I hurried over. His hair was still mussed, and he had left his hat and tie in his escape.

"Christ, you had me scared half to death," I said.

"*You* were scared? I wake up to the police banging on your door, and you're nowhere to be found? Ten years off my life!"

"Sorry, I had to see Vern. What's going on?"

"Shh shh. I don't know. I snuck out when the police left to get your landlord to unlock the door."

"But what are they doing here?" I peered up at my window. I could see shadows moving, but we were too far away to hear anything. *Maybe if I went back to the stoop...*

Sev pulled me back by my sleeve. "Oh, no you don't. I'm not letting you go to prison."

"Only if they find something."

"Believe me, they'll find something if they want to."

"Well, what do they want? Did Bella do this?"

He shrugged. "She used to send the police after rival speakeasies, but that was a long time ago–"

Something metallic smashed. *My typewriter*! The typewriter I'd bought with every penny I'd saved since childhood. That was it, that was the last thing they could ruin, and they'd done it.

"*Caro*, let's go to the train station right now–"

"No!" I pulled away from him. "I said it to Vern and I'm going to say it to you. I'm not leaving this city until I find out who killed Donnie. Because they're the same person who killed Ferri, and if we find who killed Ferri, then Bella might..."

The sword dangling over our heads hung there for a moment as Sev stared. Then he smiled and put a hand on my cheek. "*Sei troppo coraggioso.*"

"I can't help but think you just said I'm being stupid."

"No. I said you're being brave."

Harlow yelled something, and I glanced at the window. Still nothing. But Harlow being angry meant he hadn't gotten what he wanted, which was good news for me. But what had he come for? I told Sev to stay in the alley until I signaled for him, and went back inside.

I met Harlow and his goons on the staircase. "So," I said, "*now* can I know what you're doing here?"

He bared his teeth, then shouldered past me, backing me into the wall. "Spent it already, I bet," I heard him mutter as he stumped down the stairs.

Spent what? Did he think I kept a year's salary in my sock drawer like Donnie had?

They hadn't even bothered to close my door, and the mess they'd made was visible from the hall. I sighed as I picked my way through the debris. I didn't own much, but they'd put their grubby hands on every single thing. My desk and dresser drawers were all pulled out and emptied, and there were chips where they'd scraped around looking for false bottoms. My bed had been stripped and mattress handled so aggressively that the stuffing spilled out small tears. Even my clothes had been handled and dumped, all the pockets turned out, including the jacket I'd worn last night. Apparently they hadn't been too concerned with the suspicious stains. To my surprise and delight, my typewriter was only jolted out of alignment. Fixable once I found the money to get the repairs done.

I got to the window, scanned the street to make sure Harlow wasn't sticking around, and waved at Sev to come up. He arrived at my door within minutes. When he saw the chaos, he closed his eyes and rubbed at the bridge of his nose.

"*Dio*," he muttered. "They're like children, never cleaning up after themselves."

I shrugged as I put my alarm clock back on the nightstand. It had a crack running through the face and had stopped at ten-forty. Sev shut the door and grabbed clothes off the floor and folded them. He reached the stained jacket I'd been wearing last night and stopped moving mid-fold.

"Alex!" He held it out. "This is covered in blood!"

"Yeah, I know," I answered. "Lucky me, they're so dumb they didn't notice."

Sev frowned. "I don't think you're that lucky."

I stared at the jacket. He was right. Whatever Harlow had been looking for, he was so intent on it that he'd ignored evidence of violence. But if it *had* been money, who even thought I had any?

Sev shoved the jacket into my hands. "Burn it. Or throw it in the river. Just get rid of it before they come back."

I nodded. He would know how to get rid of evidence, after all. "River's better. Mr. Blake would notice if I started setting fires in–"

"Dawson!"

My name rattled against the loose floorboard slats, followed by pounding on the stairs. Could that be Harlow back again? I pushed Sev out of the way and all but charged into the hall. If Harlow wanted to fight, I was ready to oblige him. The typewriter had been the last straw.

But it wasn't Harlow. Taggart was standing on the stair landing. He wore a flat cap pulled down so his face was in shadow, but I recognized his beefy frame anywhere. He held something in his hand. Another bottle, no doubt.

"I told you to stay away from my girl," he growled.

"I have," I replied.

"Then where's she been the last two nights?"

I didn't answer. Even if I told him the truth—that Pearl had been staying with Bella Bellissima—he wouldn't believe me. But evidently my silence wasn't what he wanted to hear because he lunged at me.

Unlike our dust-up at the gymnasium, this time, he was fast. Almost too fast for me to notice the thing in his hand was a knife aimed at my stomach. I swept my arm down to block it. The blade was sharp enough to cut through my sleeve. I yelped as a line of fire blazed down my forearm.

Something blurred in the corner of my eye. I blinked to find Sev had Taggart by the front of his shirt. He slammed the boxer against the opposite wall, jarring the knife out of his hand. I wouldn't have thought Sev and his dancer's build could have knocked around someone of Taggart's bulk, but one look at his face... His gold eyes shone maliciously as his own knife flickered into his hand. This was Sev the mobster.

"I swear to God," he hissed, "if you so much as breathe near him again, I will cut a hole in you so deep that they will need miners to find the end."

Taggart whimpered. The smell of urine overlaid the scent of alcohol. Sev smiled, but it was the callous toothiness of a shark. I believed his threat. The last thing I needed was for my new boyfriend to end up charged with murder—*again*—so I grabbed Sev under the arms and hauled him back. He struggled and swore. Taggart bolted back down the stairs.

"Let me go!" Sev snarled.

"Don't be stupid! Do you want to go to prison again?"

He relaxed, and I let him go. He turned to face me, panting, his eyes still cold as they raked over me. Then his whole face thawed into concern. He made a small sound and gestured at my arm. I looked. My first thought was that my last jacket had been ruined. My second one was that that was an awful lot of blood.

"It's not that bad," I said, tugging the frayed edges of my sleeve to cover the worst of it. I tried to smile so he'd be reassured, but the pain pushed my molars together so it ended up as more of a grimace.

Sev forced his own smile, no longer sharklike, but still not up to its usual standards. "Right. Well, your doctor friend is still in business, yes? Bella didn't burn his house down?"

"No, he's around. He might be sleeping, but–"

"*Bene.*" He closed his own knife and retrieved Taggart's from the floor. He slipped them both into his pants pocket. "Let's pay him a visit."

"I don't know, Sev. After last night..."

He took a hold of my other arm with such force that I knew *no* wasn't an answer he was going to take. "Just for a minute to have a look. For my sake."

While it would have been wiser to move fast, Taggart's thunderous entrance and exit had probably already disturbed the other residents, and more noise would land me as the subject of a complaint. As much as I needed somewhere else to live, I didn't like the idea of being homeless while I was looking. Sev and I made it down the stairs in relative quiet, but at the bottom I tripped on the last step and landed hard.

"Is that you, Mr. Dawson?"

Sev turned to me, his face ashen.

"Go, it's just my landlord," I whispered. "I'll meet you outside."

Mr. Blake called my name again. "Mr. Dawson!"

"Coming!" I pushed Sev toward the door and ducked toward the shared parlor, careful to stay in the hall with my hands clamped behind my back so he wouldn't see my newest injury.

Mr. Blake sat in his armchair like a king on his throne, a newspaper across his knees like a blanket. He peered at me from behind enormous tortoiseshell glasses. "What was all that with the police?" he demanded.

"I don't know," I answered. Technically true.

Mr. Blake looked me up and down with narrowed eyes. "How do you not know, Dawson?"

Shit. "I, um..." What could I say that might justify the police coming around, but not get myself evicted? My eyes wandered, looking for a solution. They landed on Sev, who had ignored the part about meeting me outside and stood frozen by the balustrade. "I got mixed up with a girl," I said, turning back to Mr. Blake. "But she's, uh..." I dropped my voice. "Turns out she was loose. I didn't want to say anything, obviously, but–"

Mr. Blake held up a hand. I prayed my lie had been convincing. "Well, that explains Miss O'Malley's complaint. Look," he said, "I know you're lonely since Mr.

Kemp passed on, and that you're only young once, and what sins you get up to is between you and the Lord, but you *cannot*," he jabbed a finger in my direction, "I repeat, *cannot* be bringing prostitutes into the house. Understand me?"

"Absolutely, sir. Never again. Learned my lesson. I'll never bring a girl around again." Out of the corner of my eye, I saw Sev smirk.

"Good," grumbled Mr. Blake. "And who was that man running around looking for you just now?"

"That was Mr. Taggart looking for his daughter." Also technically true.

Mr. Blake settled back into his chair. "The little girl with the cat? Turns up with bruises all the time?"

"Yes, sir."

He shook his head and tutted. "I pity that family. But you stay out of that too. No good can come from meddling."

I nodded and stepped away before he could say anything else, then hustled out the door with Sev trailing behind me like a concerned hen. The pain in my arm was almost blinding now, and the steady, sticky flow of blood had made me unsteady. Martin was getting another nighttime emergency, whether he liked it or not.

Chapter Seventeen

I WAS SURPRISED to see the lights still on at Martin's house. It was very late, and between all the excitement of the night before, his general weak constitution, and his desire to keep his electricity bill as low as possible, I had expected him to be dead asleep. We stumbled through the gate, and Sev yanked open the screen door to knock on the wooden one.

No one answered.

I glanced at my arm. *I wonder how long it takes to bleed to death?*

Sev pounded again and shouted. My mind turned over many awful possibilities. Maybe Bella had taken her anger out on a helpless man. Maybe Taggart had come by and done some damage before coming to my place. Or maybe Martin had finally keeled over due to poor nutrition.

At last, the door opened. Martin gaped. "What's happened now?"

"Someone came after him with a knife," Sev answered as he pushed me inside.

"Taggart," I clarified. "He was looking for Pearl. He didn't come here, right?"

Martin shook his head. "No, thank God."

Sev looked at me, then at Martin, then back again. "Who is this Taggart?" he demanded. "What is his business with you?"

In all the mayhem, I'd forgotten to tell Sev about my fight with Taggart earlier that week. "He's Pearl's dad," I said. "You remember the little girl who was in here last night that Bella held on to? The one who you met in my apartment? Her." I winced as Martin started peeling my jacket off. "It's a long story, but in my opinion, Pearl is better off with Bella."

"I doubt that," Sev said. "You don't know what Bella is capable of."

"Well you just saw what Taggart's capable of!"

"Argue about it later," snapped Martin.

He twisted my arm to examine my injury, sending pain shooting up to my shoulder and leaving ink smeared on my skin. Ink? His right hand was covered in it, and so was the cuff of his shirt, like a pen had broken while he was holding it. But what had he been writing at this hour? He wasn't trying to make money doing it, like me.

"All right, wash up. I'll be right back," he said, then rushed into the hall.

I turned on the sink and let cold water run over my arm. Searing pain echoed from my fingers to my shoulder, and I swore using every cuss word I knew. Sev sat and watched me, his foot tapping on the tile.

"Easy, you'll put a hole in the floor," I mumbled as I inspected the gash in the light. It was still spouting a lot of blood, but more because it was long rather than deep. I wondered vaguely if I would save everybody a lot of trouble if I died of blood poisoning. "Thanks for grabbing him, by the way."

"You're the only thing I've got left, *caro*," Sev murmured. "Did you think I was going to let you get killed?"

Martin came back into the room with his bag and dropped it on the table. He muttered something about how I was lucky as he pulled bottles, needles, and dressings out of it. He glanced at the cut again before washing his hands. The water ran gray.

"You're all right," he said. "He just nicked a vein. If he'd gotten the artery we'd be in trouble. I'd still like to stitch it up though." He sat me in the other chair and laid my arm on the table. He glanced at Sev. "It's easier if I sit..."

Sev jumped up and dragged the chair over. "Of course!"

"Thank you." Martin kept looking at him. "You look familiar. Were you here last night with that woman?"

"Guilty, I'm afraid."

Martin turned his attention back to me. "I thought we talked about staying away from these..." He squinted at Sev. "These hooligans."

"Well, this hooligan just saved my life so—" I lost my train of thought as he smeared iodine over my arm. It stung like hell, and I swore again.

Martin let the subject of Sev's presence drop as he stitched. Good. I didn't want to have to explain my love life, not right then. Martin kept giving him odd looks, though. Maybe he was putting the pieces together on his own. Then again, maybe he was just justifiably nervous about a gangster in his kitchen.

After a minute or so of silence, he asked, "So, where *is* Pearl?"

"I saw her an hour or so ago," I answered. "She's safe for the night. At least I'm pretty sure." I looked at Sev, who looked away.

Martin nodded. "Good, good. Sorry. I just realized I hadn't seen her in a while. I was writing, and I didn't even notice what time it was until you came in."

Writing. My brain clicked. The suspicious letters. The rifle. No, that couldn't be it. Could it? Just because he was writing and had a rifle didn't mean he'd murdered anyone. And yet... There would be no harm in checking, right? I'd just take something Martin had written and bring it to the *Journal* office and compare it to the letters, and it wouldn't match and everything would be fine.

I looked up at Sev over Martin's shoulder. At first, I thought I could get him to sneak into the den to steal a sample, but it would require telling him, aloud, a lot of information. And anyway he wouldn't know what he was looking for. I'd have to do it myself. But I would still need his help. Sev saw the change in my expression and looked at me questioningly. I glanced at Martin, but he was still concentrating on the needle.

"When he's done," I mouthed, "distract him."

Sev's brows knit together, but he nodded. At least he was willing.

Martin started wrapping bandages around my arm. "Come back in a few days so I can check it again. In the meantime, no lifting, no pushing, no punching. No... knife fights. And keep the hell away from Pearl's father. I mean it, Alex!"

"Yeah, all right. Thanks." I rotated my arm as I stood. It still hurt, but I trusted his work. "I'm not sure how I'm going to pay you back for this."

He shook his head. "Pay me by staying out of trouble, all right? Now, I think we all need some rest."

It was going to be then or never if I was going to get a paper, wasn't it? "Actually, could I use your bathroom? Nerves."

Martin shrugged. "By all means. But God help you if you get those bandages wet."

I gave Sev a look as I walked from the kitchen. When I passed into the hallway, I heard him say, "While he's busy, *dottore*, I have a question to ask you..."

I walked as casually as I could into the hall, then swung a hard left and made a beeline for the den. Everything was more or less the same as yesterday, except the spilled ink bottle had been replaced with a fountain pen with a cracked tip. Sev and I must have startled him into breaking it with all our banging at the door in the middle of the night.

I couldn't take the top page—Martin would notice if what he'd been working on had vanished—so I picked one of the other papers at random. I tugged at the edge sticking out. I would have just lifted the whole thing, except the pen was still leaking. Going to the bathroom and coming back with ink stains on my hands would be hard to account for. At first it wouldn't give, and I wondered how long Sev could keep a story going for, but at last the paper slipped out. I jammed it into my pants pocket and got out of there.

I bolted to the bathroom and ran the water for a few seconds. I hoped everything sounded genuine in case Martin wasn't paying much attention to whatever Sev was telling him. As I came back, I heard Martin speaking in a low voice but couldn't make out what he was saying. He stopped as soon as I stepped into the room. He looked flustered, and Sev's cheeks had turned a dusty red.

"Did I miss something?" I asked.

Sev swept my jacket off the back of the chair and held it out to me. "Not a thing. Let's go!" He nodded at Martin but didn't look him in the eye. "Thank you again."

"Yeah, uh, thanks," I said as I took the jacket from him. "I meant it about paying you back. Next time I sell a story–"

Martin waved his hand. "Don't worry about it."

He held the door open, and Sev just about ran out it. I paused a moment to finagle my maimed arm into the sleeve. Just as I managed to get it on, Martin held me back.

"Just one more thing, Alex."

"Look, I'm *so* sorry to get you mixed up in this," I said. The paper from his desk felt awkward balled up in my pocket. "I'm just... It's for Donnie. If it had been anybody else, I would've let it go. But you understand, right?"

Martin opened his mouth, then shut it again and sighed. "I do. I know what it is to do...crazy things for something you believe in. Trust me. But it's dangerous, and you need to be prepared in case it backfires."

I nodded but didn't reply. I just stared at his haggard face, wondering if I could see a killer in it.

"But that isn't what I wanted to say," he continued. He inclined his head toward Sev, who was already waiting at the gate. "Have you...been intimate with that man?"

My heart raced. *No, please, not more trouble. Not tonight.* "Excuse me?"

Martin rolled his eyes and crossed his arms over his chest. "I'm not an idiot. I was in the trenches; I was a doctor. I've seen everything, and I stopped judging long ago. But as your friend and your medical counsel, I do want you to be safe. I know people who can get cheap prophylactics. All you have to do is ask."

Not the direction I'd been expecting the conversation to go in, but as long as it wasn't about people being knifed or shot, I was willing to at least play along. "I...will think about it. In the morning."

"Look, Alex, this isn't a pleasant talk for me either..."

I dashed out the door and down the porch stairs. "Bye! And thanks again!"

"I meant it about no strenuous activity!" he shouted after me.

I felt my face heat as Sev and I escaped out the back gate. We got a good block away before I burst out laughing. "What did you tell him?"

"You told me to distract him! I had to tell him something he'd believe."

"You told him you had the clap, didn't you?"

He cringed. "...Maybe. But it kept him out of your hair, didn't it? What did you do anyway?"

I pulled the paper I'd stolen out of my pocket. It was covered in neat writing, though I couldn't quite make out the actual words in the dark. I stopped giggling. Nothing quite like murder to sober you up. "Carlisle got some threatening letters. So did John Rutherford. Vern has them now. So I'm going to take this to him to compare."

Sev's eyes widened in mild horror. "That kind man? You don't actually—"

"No, no!" I protested. "...At least, I don't think so. But better to rule him out, right?"

He glanced back at the house, then at me. I couldn't read his expression. Then his mouth curved up into a half smile. "Yes, much better." He scanned the street for other people and, when he was satisfied we wouldn't be seen, looped his arm around my uninjured one and leaned his head on my shoulder. "We still have to clean."

I groaned. I'd forgotten about the mess Harlow had left. "Well, the bed is the only thing I need to do tonight. The rest can wait until morning." I made a face at the prospect of lifting a mattress with my injury. So much for no strenuous activity.

Sev shook his head. "You know he said not to overwork yourself. I'll do it."

"It's got holes in it now though. You really want to sleep on that?"

He shrugged. "Better than the floor. Besides, *caro*," he hopped up on his toes to kiss my cheek, "I'll sleep anywhere with you."

Chapter Eighteen

I HAD JUST put on my shoes when the knocking started. Sev, already up, dressed, and inspecting the holes in the mattress to see if they could be repaired, froze. I gestured, and he slipped behind the door. Remembering how Pearl had spotted him, I checked the floor for his shadow before stepping into the hall.

Harlow stood there with his chest all puffed up and a smug smile on his face. Two officers blocked the stairs down. Seeing him, I was grateful I hadn't put a jacket on yet. All of mine were bloodstained, and it would be much harder to conceal the spatters in the daylight.

"Can I help you?" I asked, pulling my door closer behind me.

"We're going to need you to come down to the station," he said.

"What for?"

He took a step forward, but I held my ground. "Seems there was another unfortunate death last night."

My heart pounded. Did Taggart get to Martin after I left? "Who?"

"A man by the name of Bert Taggart," said Harlow. "One of your neighbors, I believe." He grinned maliciously. "One you had an altercation with a few days ago."

Taggart? My panicked mind flickered through memories of the night before. Had Sev stabbed him and I didn't see?

"How?" I croaked. *Great, now you sound guilty.*

Harlow extended a hand like it was a friendly invitation. "Why don't we go down to the station and talk about it?"

I swallowed and resisted the urge to peek back into my room to check on Sev. "What if I don't want to go?"

"Oh, you're *going*, Dawson. Your choice about how quietly."

I glanced at the two other cops. I could probably take on Harlow alone, but with all that back-up? Never. And what if Sev got involved again? What if the cops shot him?

I closed the door the rest of the way. "In that case, I would love to go down to the station with you."

THEY DUMPED ME in an interview room deep inside the station, far away from any windows. The walls and floor were rough cement, and it was bare of furniture except for a table, a chair, and a single over-bright light. I couldn't place the smell at first. Mold and...rot? Maybe a mouse had died in one of the dark corners. They slammed the iron door closed.

I sat and tried to make sense of everything, but I lost my concentration in the dungeon-like atmosphere. The light burned my eyes, and its electrical buzz drowned out every sound beyond the room. It threaded through my head, making it ache. I lost sense of time. Had it been a half hour? Longer? Maybe they were planning on leaving me alone overnight.

My thoughts wavered between logic and suspicion. Had Sev stabbed Taggart? I couldn't remember his actions exactly, only his vicious smile. There had been an awful lot of blood, but it had all been mine. Right? What if Taggart had gone after Martin, and Martin killed him in self-defense? Unlikely. Martin could barely defend himself against a strong gust of wind. And if Martin had killed him, why had the cops come to me? Had *I* done something? If I couldn't remember Sev doing something, could I forget what I'd done too?

Get it together, Alex. This is what they want to happen.

I had to do something to focus. I patted my clothes. No cigarettes. I was still bumming them off Sev. No notebook. But what was the papery ball? I pulled it out. It was the handwriting sample I'd stolen from Martin. I'd never taken it out. I stuffed it back into my pocket in case someone came in.

It was a good thing I did because the door screeched open a few seconds later. Harlow lumbered in and smacked his hands on the metal table. I flinched at the resulting bang, and he grinned.

"Scared, huh? Funny, I wouldn't have thought a big guy like you would be afraid of a little noise."

I took a deep breath before answering. "I'm trying to be cooperative. Maybe you should do the same and tell me what happened to Bert Taggart."

"Why are you in such a rush? You don't have to go to work. Your employer is dead, in case you forgot."

I thought about arguing that I did have other work, but Harlow was the sort of person who believed that writing wasn't a real job. Anyway, talking back wouldn't be wise.

Harlow straightened and began to pace a circle around me and the table. "Your neighbor Albert Taggart was shot with a rifle outside his place of business last night around eleven."

I raised my head, relief loosening my shoulders. Not stabbed. Not Sev. But that still had Martin on the hook. Not that I thought Martin would shoot anyone. Then again, if he thought both Pearl and me were in danger... What time had I been over there?

"So, why are you coming to me?" I asked. "Taggart was a drunk and a bully. Made a lot of enemies."

"Yes, but not all enemies attacked him a few days ago."

Sweat accumulated on my back and made my shirt sticky. "Where'd you hear that?"

"Someone happened to mention it when we responded to the call last night."

"Did they say it was me?"

"They described a man who sounded an awful lot like you, and I thought, huh, I was just at Dawson's place."

"Yeah, and I was cleaning my room after you sacked it, if your next question is what I was doing last night."

"About that. When we came to your building this morning, we talked to your landlord first, and he said that Taggart came by, left, and that you followed after him in a hurry."

Damn. "He did, and I did leave soon after, but I was only going to a friend's place."

"That late at night?"

I stayed silent, unable to find an answer that wouldn't incriminate me or Martin, or both. I could mention Sev, but then I would have to say where they could find him, and that would lead to more suspicion. And when they questioned him, he might not think to lie, and if he did, his story wouldn't match mine. Could I say Vern? Would Vern even step up for me?

Harlow stopped circling me. "I want an answer."

I stayed silent.

Harlow growled and started pacing again, like a lion considering the best way to go in for the kill. He made it one lap, then kicked the table. I winced as the edge hit my rib. I wondered how long it would take for him to notice the stitches in my arm, and if that would give him ideas. How many years would I get if I fought back?

Someone hammered on the door, then opened it a crack. An officer poked his head in. "Sir? Someone is here to speak with you."

Harlow's brow furrowed, but either curiosity or worry got the better of him because he started for the door. It closed with a heavy clang, followed by a scrape as the bolt was drawn.

I sighed, thankful for the break. A few minutes was all I needed to get myself in order and avoid a beating. I was a writer, after all. I made money creating convincing stories. The trouble would be hanging all the pretty lies on the framework that had been given to me.

Harlow had said Taggart had been killed with a rifle. He could have made that up, but it seemed an odd thing to lie about, especially when he could have said nothing at all. So, the rifle was the linchpin. And since this was the third murder scene involving one—fourth if they were counting Bella's near miss outside the church—the cops were probably very nervous now. Same method probably meant the same person. And while they couldn't pin Ferri's death on me, they knew I was there when Carlisle died, and now here I was, close to Taggart's. They would have been stupider than usual not to pull me in. Even if I hadn't pulled the trigger, in their minds I must have known the person who had. But did I? Who in the world would go after Carlisle, Bella, and a run-of-the-mill bastard like Taggart? What did the three of them have in common?

The door opened again, revealing Harlow, and my stomach dropped. *Out of time.*

But he just stood there. "You're free to go," he grumbled.

"What?"

He repeated himself and stepped out of the doorway to clear my exit. Suspicious, I stood and edged toward him. I hesitated at the threshold, half sure I was going to get that thick door slammed onto my foot or hand, but he just glared as I passed him. Strange, but I wasn't about to question my luck.

He escorted me to the front desk of the precinct. Martin was there, clutching Pearl's tiny hand. He was shaking; she seemed indifferent.

"Oh, thank God," Martin exclaimed, releasing Pearl to hug me. "As soon as I heard what happened, I came right down to tell them you were with me when he was killed."

I returned the embrace, but my mind started sorting through the threads. *Had* I been with Martin at the time? Was he lying to protect me? Or maybe he was protecting himself? The paper with his handwriting on it felt heavy in my pocket.

I knelt down so I could look Pearl in the eye. "You all right?" I asked.

She nodded but said nothing as she lunged for a hug. Something smacked into my back as she did. When she pulled away, I saw it was a new, good-quality rag doll. A gift from Bella?

"I think she's in shock," Martin whispered as I straightened. "The police just brought her over to me an hour ago, saying she refused to talk to anyone else. But I can't get a straight story out of her. Something about staying with a princess? I asked and the police said she could stay with me for a few days so she'll calm down, but after that…"

"We'll figure it out," I said, eyeing Harlow, who hovered a few yards away with an expression that could have soured milk. "Let's just go."

Martin glanced at Harlow, then headed for the exit as quickly as he could while dragging a little girl. "They didn't hurt you again, right?" he muttered as we made it outside to the noon sun.

"No, but you had great timing because they were about to."

"Well, they kept me waiting long enough. I must have been there an hour begging to see you before they let you out." Martin clicked his tongue and shook his head. "Something needs to be done about these monsters. I'm not sure who's worse, the gangs or the people who are supposed to protect us from them."

His words rattled down my spine. Had he always said stuff like that, vague but angry barbs at corrupt forces? It sounded too much like those letters. I jammed my hand in my pocket to touch the paper I'd stolen from him. I just needed to get to Vern so I could compare the paper to the letters and get some relief from the suspicion hanging over my head.

"Anyway, thanks for coming so fast," I said. "But if you don't mind, I'm going to head home. Get some sleep or something."

"By all means," Martin answered. "I know this hasn't been an easy week for you. But please, if you need anything, come to the house. I'll help any way I can."

I forced a smile. "I know. You're a good friend."

GOING DOWN TO the *Journal* building was a bit of a blur. In fact, I ended up missing the stop. I only realized it when I saw those bleak angel statues glare down at me as the trolley zipped by. So, I ended up doubling back. It struck me as kind of amusing. If someone was following me, I'd probably just really confused them.

When I got to the newsroom, Vern waved me over. I tugged on my sleeve, making sure my bandages were hidden. Running around without a jacket I might be able to explain, but stitches would provoke questions.

"I thought you were going to come in first thing," said Vern as he scanned me. "What happened to your jacket?"

"They're all either torn up or stained," I replied. "The police raided my apartment last night and dragged me in this morning." I was getting good at this half truth thing. "Bert Taggart's dead."

"I heard!" Vern leaned in and lowered his voice. "Word is, he was shot by a marksman. Know anything about that?"

"Uh, maybe. But first, can I see those letters again?"

"Right, sure."

He pulled open a drawer and laid all three out next to each other. I took the paper out of my pocket and smoothed it out on the blotter, keeping my hand over most of the script. I didn't want to see. But there was no avoiding it now. I lifted my hand. The handwriting and the paper matched the letter the *Journal* had gotten and the one from Rutherford's office.

Vern stared at it, then at me. "Where'd you get that?"

I found my mouth had run dry. I had to be imagining it, seeing things that weren't really there due to exhaustion and stress.

He picked up Martin's paper and the matching letters. "These are almost word for word. I need to know where you found this."

"Martin's," I squeaked, too dumbfounded to lie.

"Your friend?" Realization dawned on his face. "You wanted to know about his arrest. I found it last night. It was for a protest. A political protest. Socialism."

"Yeah. But that...that doesn't mean anything. What about the other letter? Two different people, right? What if–"

"Alex, you were the one who thought they were connected to–"

"Well I changed my mind! Martin isn't dangerous. He's...he's... He's a doctor. Doctors don't hurt people."

"Yeah? Ever heard of H. H. Holmes? Linda Hazzard? Thomas Cr–"

"Why do you have to do this, huh?" I snapped. "Why do you have to think the worst of everyone?"

He jabbed a finger at me. "Because naïve suckers like you get ripped apart. You and your innocent genius thought, yeah, I'll just talk to Bella Bellissima. How bad can that go? Well now you know. There're already a bunch of dead bodies, and maybe more coming because you don't want to admit that one of your friends could be hiding things from you. Not everybody is an angel and plays by the rules. Just accept it."

I didn't know how to answer that. In my silence, I could feel other people's eyes on us. Pain spasmed up my injured arm as my hands balled into fists. Had Martin really gone and shot someone after he'd taken the time to sew me up? Had he really shot Ferri, then tried to save his life ten minutes later?

Ten minutes later. That was it.

"He couldn't have done it!" I declared. "The police said Taggart died at the gym around eleven." I pulled up the cuff of my sleeve so Vern could see the bandages. "My clock stopped at ten-forty and I got hurt right after that and had to go to him. Even if I left Martin's before eleven, there's no way he could have gotten all the way downtown by then. Even if he took a cab, which he can't because he can't afford one!"

Vern blinked at my injury. "How did *that* happen?"

"Not important. What's important is that Martin couldn't have shot Bert Taggart. End of story."

"Doesn't mean he didn't do the others, Dawson. Or didn't know about them ahead of time." He tapped the letter Emma had given me. "More than one person, remember? Maybe it was the other one. Maybe they're in cahoots."

How dare he? I had just told him why Martin was innocent, and yet he kept refuting it. "Well how do I know it's not you?" I demanded. "More dead people means more stories, which means you get to keep your job. Move up in the world. Get out of this stupid corner and have a real office. Save your brother and sister and all that?"

"Are you sure you want to go down that alley? You want to start accusing your friends?"

"You just tried to make me accuse Martin! I know what it looks like, but he's not connected to any of it. I bet Taggart never got anything even resembling these. And anyway, angry letters aren't a proof of anything. If everyone who got angry killed someone, there'd be no one left!"

Everyone was definitely staring now. I shrank into myself, embarrassed and worn out. Vern folded his hands and placed them on top of his desk.

"Are you done throwing a tantrum now?" he asked.

I looked at the floor, my anger already flooding away. "Um, yeah. Sorry."

"Good, because you need to save that energy for getting the real story." He collected the papers and stuffed them back in the drawer. "I won't write about this, you have my word. But I need you to promise me something in return." He settled back in his chair. "Keep your eyes open. There's still a shooter on the loose."

"I'm doing my best," I said.

"Do better," Vern replied. "So far, your best just gets people dead."

Chapter Nineteen

I STUMBLED THROUGH the door of my building, sweaty and disheveled after the cycle of panic and relief I'd gone through. My only thoughts were of rest and of the joyful expression on Sev's face when I unlocked the door.

But he wasn't there. My breath caught. Had he been found out? No, I wouldn't even entertain that possibility. Maybe he'd gone to the bathroom and locked himself out? I glanced down the corridor. No, even from there I could see the door opened a crack. Maybe he was pulling the door trick again, unsure if it was me? I took a tentative step into the room.

"Sev?" I called.

Nothing.

My heart slammed against my ribs as I scanned the room for any indication of where he might have gone. Then I saw a piece of paper folded on my bed. I snatched it up with shaking hands. I was almost afraid to read it, but it was so short that I basically already had: *At the Ostia—Sev*

THE WHOLE TROLLEY ride I kept thinking about all the terrible things that could have happened. Had Mr. Blake come in and seen him? The police? What if Bella sent a goon to drag him back to her? Or worse? And what if the letter was bait? While Bella hadn't tried to kill me yet, that didn't mean she wasn't planning to. After all, the Ostia was a great place for murder.

I skidded through the back door of the club in a near panic, but nothing about the backstage seemed odd. People wandered around indifferent to my presence like they had the last time I was there. But that didn't mean someone wasn't hiding in the crowd, waiting to strike.

"Alex!"

My knees nearly gave out in relief when I saw Sev by one of the dressing room doors. He had cleaned up a little, even had a shave and a change of clothes. It took every ounce of willpower I had to keep myself from just running to him and smothering him in kisses on the spot.

"Christ, don't ever do that to me again! Cryptic notes, what were you thinking?"

"I'm sorry, I was in a hurry." He patted my arm. "You look like you're dying. Here, sit." He dragged me a few yards to a folding chair by a restroom.

I let myself collapse. "I thought we wanted to stay far away from Bella?"

He shrugged. "The police took you, and I didn't know what else to do. She has ties inside, I thought she could get you out. Didn't she?"

"No," I said. "They let me go when Martin came by and told them I was with him when Taggart was killed."

"As if they'd cave to such a feeble excuse," someone said.

I wouldn't even have known it was Bella except for her voice. She came out of the rotating crowd, raven-like in a plain black dress. No jewelry, no makeup, no fur. Her hair was pulled back in simple rolls and covered with a black lace kerchief. She fiddled with something in her hand: a rosary with blue ceramic beads.

I watched her suspiciously. "*You* called them off?"

She shrugged. "A captain owed me a favor."

So, that was why Harlow had rushed me out of there. I should've known it wasn't logic that set me free. "Why?"

She tossed her head. Even at the end of her rope she was still proud. Queens had to carry on without their consorts. "Since my darling cousin as well as your *gattina* have both insisted that you are hunting the man who..." she hesitated over the word, "...murdered Dario, your eternal punishment can wait. And by the way, I was offended you'd think I would try to hurt your doctor friend. Think me ruthless if you must, but I am not unreasonable."

Anger flamed again. Did she think she could talk down to me like I was another simpering crony? I was about to snap at her, but Sev caught my eye. His lips thinned as his gaze passed between Bella and me. I took a breath. My own safety wasn't the only one I had to think about.

"Sure," I said slowly. "I want to find the murderer. But I'm going to need to talk to people here."

Bella's shoulders relaxed. Had she been worried I'd refuse to help her? "You can ask anything of these people with my blessing. And they will tell the truth." She shifted the rosaries to her other hand. They clacked together almost as loudly as her jewelry had. "In here, *I* am the law."

I glanced at Sev. He smiled. "She's very sorry about scaring us the other night and wants to make it up to us."

I doubted that, but as I hadn't been killed outright, I figured it was safe to stay. "Can I talk to the singers from that night again?"

Bella nodded. "I thought you might, so I had them wait. Come." She gestured at Sev as he made to follow us. "*You* stay here."

He froze like an obedient dog. I held my tongue.

She led the way back to the dressing room I remembered as Molly's. Both she and Birdie were there, in street clothes this time. Molly looked sour, but that might have been because her meal ticket of shaking down Sev had been eliminated. No point in blackmail now that everybody knew. Lucille smiled, but now I could see how vapid and empty it was. I wondered why they had agreed to talk now. Had Bella threatened them? Bribed them? Or did they just feel bad now that two murders had turned into five?

"Ladies," I said as I squeezed into the space between the back of the chairs and the costume rack.

Part of a feather boa fell across my shoulder, and some fluff went up my nose. I sneezed, my body jolting so hard it hit the rack. More costumes and props fell on top of me as I crumpled against the fresh pain in the bruise Harlow had inflicted on my ribs. Bella ignored me by mouthing the words of prayers she clearly wasn't concentrating on.

Birdie, on the other hand, giggled. "The nosy one is back!" she exclaimed.

"Is that what I'm known as around here?" I mumbled.

"Not the only thing, but the others are naughty."

Molly put a cigarette in her mouth and scowled. "What do you want to know? I told you I didn't see anything the first time you were here."

Bella spun one of the beads. "Tell them about who would come backstage."

"Lots of people come backstage," Molly answered. "That giant lug was here the day the mayor was killed. You're here now." She gave Bella a sidelong glance. "Romano. Ciretti. Even Dario would come around sometimes..."

Bella straightened, and the whole room turned to ice. "Do not test me. I may have let you and the other girls have free rein here for a long time, but I assure you, I will have no problems getting rid of who I think it's too much trouble to keep. And I hear that it's hard to find new work nowadays."

Molly's mouth clamped shut.

I decided to stop being subtle. I wanted to get out of this mess as fast as possible. "Birdie, you said you were having an affair with Carlisle."

Her nose crinkled as she smiled that waxwork grin of hers. "It is not an affair if he pays you, yes?"

Of course. I didn't know why it hadn't occurred to me before. They were prostitutes, not just singers. If Carlisle had been infatuated with Birdie and had to pay to see her every time, it would explain why he was hemorrhaging money.

"So, Carlisle was... paying you to sleep with him?"

"Yes, but he didn't mind." She winked. "Roy liked me so much he said he would leave his wife for me and take me away from here."

"Did he really?"

She shrugged. "Many men say that to me. They love me. They will pay me enough that I won't work again. They will divorce their wives. But he was the only one who would stay until morning. And the only one who brought me to his house instead of a hotel. Your friend helped with that. He said he understood what it was to sneak for love."

I flushed. She'd told me Donnie had helped Carlisle arrange the affair the first time I'd come by, but now it made a lot more sense. "Did anyone else know about this?"

Molly flicked more ash away. "You just want to know if your boyfriend knew. Hard to wrap your head around fucking someone's pimp."

The thought hadn't even crossed my mind. But now that the idea was there, I had to consider it. Had Sev lied to me about what he did for Bella? What else could he be lying about?

Birdie laughed. "Oh, he scares easy, doesn't he? Look, he's gone white."

"*Basta.*" Bella drew everyone's attention again without even shouting. "Teasing him does not help anyone." She looked at me. "Severo is like you, too nice to know when something's happening in front of his face. The girls are *my* project." Another bead clicked menacingly. "It is women's work, after all."

Molly snorted. "Project? Is that what you're calling it now?"

"When I hired you, I told you what was expected, and you agreed anyway. Did you just think just your pretty voice was going to get you anywhere? Vaudeville is dying and the liquor routes dried up, so get used to the new order."

"Easy for you to say when you're the one on top of the heap. If I left to starve on my own, you'd just get some other dumb kid. I hear you've got one already. Little girl wearing your favor around town."

"Look," I snapped, turning to Bella. "I'm not part of whatever the hell this is, but you leave Pearl out of it."

She gasped, and the rosaries clattered together. "I would never!" She pointed at Molly. "Get out. You are done here. One hour to get your things. You." She gestured at Lucille. "Take the extra shift and an extra fifty for your trouble. And you," she rounded on me, "you finish this before I have to lose any more people. You got what you came for, so go."

"But I didn't—"

"Out!" she roared.

I stumbled over fallen costumes as I squeezed my way back out of the room. I was sure people were staring, but I just didn't care anymore. I was tired, hungry, humiliated, and terrified. And I was no closer to finding out anything than I had been.

I made my way back to the restroom looking for Sev so we could go home, but he hadn't waited there. I couldn't help but smile a little. He wasn't quite as compliant as Bella thought he was.

I wandered for a little and found myself in the wings of the stage. The stairs of the catwalk loomed next to me, half hidden from everything else by heavy curtains. I stared at the steel and wood above me. So easy to access, and probably a million sets of fingerprints. I wondered if the cops had found casings, little good that would do. You needed the gun to match ballistics. No wonder the police were having a tough time of it. But I wasn't police, so I climbed.

I had a great view of the dining floor except for the bar in the back. Some waiters and other staff were scurrying around the ordered tables laying fancy napkins and silver knives. I squinted. Where had Carlisle been sitting? It was hard to tell now that everything had been moved around. I stared for a few seconds, rearranging everything in my mind until it matched that night. His seat had been where the center of a table was now, and his head near the current edge. He'd been at the 9-o-clock position, then Emma, then Logan, then Mrs. Green. It was a very clear shot to him and Donnie both, and if anyone happened to look up, the stage lights would have been hard to see through.

Unless they were sitting at an angle. Logan and Emma would have been blinded, but not Mrs. Green. Maybe she had noticed something and not realized.

"There you are!" exclaimed Sev as he mounted the last step to the catwalk. "Bella is furious. What did you say?"

"I didn't say anything! We were talking about Carlisle sleeping with Birdie and then all of a sudden Molly's accusing Bella of prostituting Pearl and then all hell breaks loose."

He shook his head, his eyes wide. "She wouldn't do such a thing."

"Well you could've fooled me!" I growled. "She's already running God-knows what. What's wrong with everyone? Kill and be killed and no one gives a shit? How do you live like that?"

"No one said we like it," Sev answered as he leaned against the rail next to me. He pulled his cigarette case out of his pocket and offered it to me. I shook my head. He shrugged and took one for himself.

"Did you know Birdie and Molly were prostitutes?" I asked.

He turned to face the club and sighed. Smoke billowed away from him. "How much would you hate me if I said yes?"

"And you didn't think to tell me?"

"I didn't think it was important. It clearly wasn't Birdie who killed them. She doesn't have the brains."

"But it could be someone else who bought her. Someone who's jealous that she was with the mayor. You made me think it was Martin for days!"

Sev's head snapped to me. "I never made you do anything, let alone suspect your friends. Yes, I stayed silent, but what good would it have done to say? I don't know who her clients are, only she and Bella do, and neither of them would have given the names away for free. Would you have gone to every rich man's house and asked if he had fucked a red-haired French girl?"

"Maybe, yeah!"

I cringed at my weak comeback and turned away. No, I wouldn't have. Besides, being jealous didn't require an affair. All anyone needed was the idea that she was pretty enough to kill for. Or any idea really. One idea that would link Carlisle and Bella. And Taggart. That was the one that didn't make any sense. Even if the whole stupid thing had to do with boxing, why kill him now? And why bother with a rifle? A handgun at ten feet would have worked just as well.

Sev's voice interrupted my thoughts. "I want to tell you something else."

My stomach heaved as I looked at him. Nothing he was about to say could be good. "Yeah?"

"I don't know if it's important, but... I knew your friend Donnie. Not well! Just for a minute here and there when he was picking up Birdie." Sev waved his cigarette. "It was always, you know, polite conversation, but the last time I saw him before he died, he said he knew someone I would like to meet. I didn't think anything of it at the time, but," he put his hand on mine, which had turned almost white from clutching the railing so hard, "I think he meant you."

Not where I had expected the conversation to go. If it was true, it explained why Donnie had shown up early and been acting so strangely. If it was a lie... Would Sev lie just to keep me from being angry with him? Was that better or worse?

"You're making that up," I mumbled, looking away so he couldn't see the tears welling in my eyes.

"I'm not making it up." Sev ran his hand up and down my arm. "He was a nice man, and you are a nice man, and sometimes," he let his hand drop, "wonderful things come from terrible things."

I looked at him. The words should have felt empty, trite and false, but somehow they didn't when he said then. Suddenly I felt very silly standing twenty feet in the air snuffling back tears, and I had to laugh at myself.

Sev's easy smile spread across his face. "There we are. *Bene.*" He brought his hand to the back of my neck. "*Baciami.*"

That one I knew. *Kiss me.* A request I was happy to fulfill.

Someone stomped onto the stage, heels clicking on the hardwood. It was Bella, as dark and proud as Lucifer himself. She put her hands on her hips and raised her face to us. "Both of you. Down here. Now."

There are some things in the world that couldn't be argued with, and an already-upset Bella Bellissima was one of them. We all but flew down the stairs. Back on the ground, she seemed twice as annoyed. It was almost like she radiated heat. I noticed Sev lower his head in deference, but I did my best not to cower under her glare. She had invited me in, after all, and wanted the murders solved as much as I did, if not more.

She scowled at me. "I got you away from the police so you could help me, not weep and slobber all over each other."

I shrugged. I didn't have any more patience for her grandstanding. "Well, I don't imagine you did it to be kind."

The beads flashed in her hands as her eyes narrowed. She'd done the calculations already, but she was just running them again in her head to make sure. "I want the heart of the man who killed Dario. The police will not bring it to me. *You* may. Or at least you will try."

"Should I be flattered, or...?"

"Would you prefer if I tortured you into doing it? It would be easy, wouldn't it? I know where it would hurt the most." She reached out with her free hand and patted Sev's scarred cheek. He flinched.

I straightened, ready to shove her away, but Sev touched my sleeve and gave me a warning look. I let my balled hands drop to my sides. The stitches down my arm ached in response.

She smirked. "Birdie was right. You *are* easy to scare." The rosary shuffled by another bead. "I am many, *many* terrible things," she said, "but I would not kill my blood to prove a point. Nor would I sell a little girl, despite what Molly seems to think."

"Then why are you toying with Pearl?" I growled, still tense from her threats. "Why bother with her at all?"

The venom in Bella's eyes dissipated. "Do you remember I said that Dario and I had a daughter once?"

I did, vaguely. It was part of the jumble that was the night Ferri died, but it hadn't seemed all that important at the time. "Don't tell me you miss being a mother?"

She raised a shoulder, and the rosary clacked as she collected the whole thing into her fist. "I miss not having my heart in pieces."

I couldn't tell if I felt bad for her or not. She'd done horrible things, but I couldn't quite muster up the spite required to think she deserved to lose both her daughter and her husband. If she hurt even half as much as I did from losing Donnie, maybe I could forgive her at least some things.

I slipped my arm behind Sev's back and started guiding him away. "We're going."

Bella nodded. I could have sworn there were tears in her eyes. "Fine. No, wait." She put her mask back up. "Severo tells me your clothes are all ruined. I will have new ones brought to you. And things for him too. I know he did not get a chance to collect anything."

Sev bowed his head. *"Grazie. Ch'è molto gentile."*

She snorted and stormed away, her heels echoing on the hardwood of the stage. The Queen of Sin had dismissed us, at least for now.

Chapter Twenty

SOMETIME IN THE night, two suitcases were left on the steps of my boardinghouse for me. Mr. Blake had a dictionary's worth of words to say on the subject of mysterious packages, but I only half heard them over the thud of my footfalls as I hauled the damn things up three flights of stairs. I dumped them in the middle of the floor, where they took up about a third of the space, making it nearly impossible to move without tripping.

"Bella could have at least been classy about delivering these," I grumbled, rubbing my injured arm. Heavy lifting a day and a half after stitches maybe hadn't been my brightest idea. "Sent a bellhop or something."

"She could have done nothing," Sev answered as he lifted one onto the bed. The mattress was still losing filling, and I heard it rustle as the new weight was added.

"Don't tell me you forgave her?"

He was quiet for a second, then said, "She asked, so I did. I've forgiven her for other things. And she said she would let me have me job back—"

"She ruined your life!"

He popped open the suitcase and started sifting through the clothes inside without looking at me. "We can't both be unemployed, Alex, and we can't both stay here. It's too dangerous."

His calmness dug under my skin. "Well, what happened to the bookshop in India idea?"

"We'd still need money."

"I'll write!" I insisted. "I'll finish a novel. I'll start on a serial. I'll–"

"*You*," he turned and, his eyes narrowed, tossed a shirt at me, "will change into something less disgusting and be grateful for it. You can't show up to that Mrs. Green looking like a vagrant."

He had a point. Whatever else happened, I still needed to know who killed Donnie, and hopefully the old bag would be able to point me in the right direction. I put on one of the suits Bella had provided. It didn't fit right, but at least it wasn't torn or bloody, which put it miles ahead of everything of mine. Sev ignored me while I dressed, focusing instead on brushing out his own clothes.

"I mean it about the writing," I mumbled as I tugged the too-short sleeve. It barely covered my bandages. "It's not fair, you having to pay for everything."

"It's not about the money," he replied.

"Then what are we fighting about?"

His gold eyes scrutinized me. It was unnerving how much he looked like Bella when he did that. They must have inherited the same calculating stare from a grandparent. Finally, he said, "It's so easy for you, isn't it? Knowing the right and wrong thing." His gaze softened, and the crow's feet appeared. "I admire it, but I could never quite manage it on my own."

"Well you're not *bad*," I sputtered, caught off-guard by his answer. "Just, you know...things happen..."

Sev laughed. "You don't need to justify my choices to me. But I would appreciate if you didn't judge me for them either."

Heat crept up my neck. "Right. Sorry."

"I forgive you. See? So easy." He smirked, then sighed and came over to straighten my jacket. "Though I will admit she could have tried harder to find the right size. But beggars can't be choosers, I suppose."

I caught his hand and just held it against my chest. "Come down and wait for the trolley with me?"

He gave me a peck on the lips. "If it will make you happy."

I DIDN'T MIND waiting for the trolley. The weather was beautiful and bright, promising the beginning of summer, and the grassy patches next to the tracks were growing violets and clover. I slid my notebook out of my pocket to scribble something about light in the darkness as Sev talked about his plans to shuffle the Ostia's musical lineup now that Molly had been ousted.

Something banged—a car backfiring?—and my chest tightened. The world narrowed to just in front of me as my stomach pitched and blood pounded in my ears. I wobbled as the strength fled from my knees.

Sev grabbed my arm. "Are you all right?"

"I'm fine," I gasped.

He frowned. "You don't look fine." He stooped to pick up my notebook; I hadn't realized I'd dropped it. "What's wrong?"

I blinked a few times to get my bearings. The initial shock had worn off and all I was left with was a speeding heart rate and a sense of choking unease. "I'm fine," I repeated.

"I'm afraid you're not a good liar, caro. I blame your strong conscience. Come. We're going to see your doctor friend." He nudged me. At first my feet stuck to the ground, but at another gentle push, they started following his directions. "Remind me to have a gift sent to him. We're giving him too much business lately."

I didn't want to bother Martin yet again, but I couldn't deny he was needed. Why did I feel like I was going to keel over? Maybe there had been something on that knife and was only now getting to me? No, Taggart hadn't been savvy enough to think of a slow-acting poison. And anyway, I'd checked earlier that morning. The stitches were clean, the area around them barely red.

I scraped through my mind for another explanation. Everything had been normal, pleasant even, until I heard a loud noise. Actually, now that I was thinking about it, I'd been jumpy at noise lately. I'd heard of men with shell shock having breakdowns at such a measly excuse, but I hadn't sat through bombings and shootings. Actually, scratch that—I had. At least the shooting part.

A girl shrieked somewhere on the next block, and it sent chills down my spine. *Calm down, Alex. It's just some kids playing.*

Except it wasn't. The screaming didn't dissolve into laughter. "Help!" she cried.

Pearl.

My dragging feet grew wings, and I flew toward Martin's house. I didn't know I could move that fast. People on the sidewalk dodged out of the way to avoid me. I reached the alley that ran behind the houses just as Martin's gate opened. Pearl careened out of it, Daisy a black-and-orange streak behind her.

"Help!" she screamed again. She launched herself at me, grabbing my hand and pulling. "Mr. Dawson help! Mr. Martin is hurt."

I looked toward the gate, but it had swung closed, obstructing the view of the yard. I craned my neck to see over the fence. I could just make out a toppled laundry basket on the porch stairs.

Sev skidded into the alley, panting. "What's going on?"

I pushed Pearl toward him. "Stay with her. Don't follow me."

"But–"

I didn't hear the rest of what he said over the slamming of the gate.

Martin was sitting hunched with his back against the final post of the railing. For a brief, shining second I thought he had just tripped on the steps. Simply twisted an ankle or broken a wrist. Then he moved, and I saw the blood on his stomach. I hurried to his side.

"Alex?" he rasped.

"Yeah, it's me," I said as I pulled off my too-small jacket and bundled it up to press against the wound. I had no idea if that was the right thing, but the only doctor in the place was preoccupied.

"I was doing laundry..." he mumbled.

As if that made the slightest difference. He'd been shot from afar while defenseless. Like Donnie, like Ferri, like Taggart. I scanned the upper windows of the surrounding abandoned buildings, but whoever had done it was long gone. The gunfire must have been the sound that set me off. It was a small consolation that there *had* been danger; I wasn't completely losing my grip.

"Sev, call the hospital!" I shouted, hoping he heard me.

Martin grabbed my hand. It was as cold as ice and quivering as badly as my own. "Don't. They fired me," he whimpered.

He wasn't thinking straight. "That was years ago. They won't even remember."

"They will! I wouldn't..." Martin shook his head. "They got rid of me because I was arrested for dissenting... Dissenting..."

"Yeah, I know."

His brow furrowed. "How?"

"You mentioned it once," I lied. I wasn't about to tell him I'd raided his house and forced Vern to go through police records. "And you know what, it doesn't matter. They were stupid to get rid of you." *I was stupid for ever doubting you.*

He nodded, but his head drooped as soon as he stopped.

Vern's scolding voice rattled around in my head: *Your best just gets people dead.* Was that what I was doomed for, everyone I ever cared about stripped away one by one because I wasn't good enough? I glanced up at the gaping windows of the vacant houses again. Pity the killer hadn't stuck around to shoot me too.

What I couldn't get my head around was why. Carlisle, I could understand. Ferri too. Hell, I could even understand Taggart. But who would want to kill Martin, who had never done anything bad to anybody?

Except for the letters. He had sent threatening letters.

"Martin, can you hear me?" I asked as I shook him. "Why did you send threatening letters to Carlisle and Rutherford?"

That seemed to perk him up a little, and his unfocused eyes blazed like he had been waiting to give his side of the story. "They were killing us," he groaned. "Slowly. Starving us out. Just taking because they can. What'll happen to the neighborhood if no one helps?" He tried to straighten but winced and slumped again. "I just wanted to scare them into doing right by us."

"That was dumb. You'll just get in trouble like that. Who was writing them with you?"

He shook his head. "No one?" He looked over my shoulder. "Where's Pearl?" he asked. "I just saw her..."

"She's all right. Sev's got her. Martin, listen. You have to stay with us, all right? For me and her. We can't..." I swallowed to keep my tears at bay. "We can't lose anybody else."

The gate creaked open and Sev eased in. "I sent her to the payphone," he said. His eyes flickered to Martin's face, then to mine, looking for instruction.

"When she gets back, take her to Bella," I said. "She'll be able to protect her, or at least keep her comfortable until..." Until what? Until Martin was back on his feet? Unlikely. Until Bella got killed? As far as I knew, the murderer was still after her hide. "Just take care of her. Please."

He nodded. "We'll wait for you at the Ostia."

I had a few choice words to say about bringing Pearl into that place, but I didn't have the stamina or time for an argument. Martin moaned and crumpled into himself. I shook him again, but this time he didn't react. His chest still rose and fell, but I had no idea how long that might last.

I turned back to Sev. "Get her now. I don't want her seeing this."

He didn't even answer, just bolted out the gate again, leaving me alone, cradling yet another dying friend.

Chapter Twenty-One

TIME MOVED LIKE it was stuck in tar, every tick of the clock in the hospital waiting room taking a hundred years. When I wasn't staring at the clock, I was staring at my shoes. I wished for cigarettes, but I still hadn't had the chance to buy any, so I chewed my thumbnail instead, hard and long enough to take it down to the quick. I couldn't bear to look at anyone else trapped in the room with me. I knew Martin wasn't making it out of there anytime soon, but I needed to hear it from someone who had a better grip on reality than me.

A shadow moved across the floor, and I looked up, hoping it belonged to a doctor or a nurse who could give me some information. Instead it was Harlow bearing down on me.

"What is it they say about bad pennies?" he said. "Something about always turning up?"

Finally, something I could apply searing hatred to. "Yeah, it's the same thing they say about smug jackasses," I growled.

He grabbed my lapels and hauled me to my feet. "Now listen here, you disgusting little–"

"Gentlemen!" The receptionist shot up. "This is a hospital, not a boxing ring!"

He let go of me. "Then I guess we're taking this outside."

"If it's all the same, I'd like to stay here," I said. He wouldn't try pummeling me with half a dozen witnesses around. Right? "Unless you have a good reason to arrest me this time." I put my wrists in front of him, poised to be cuffed. He scowled. I laughed—a half-hysterical giggle—and let my arms drop. "You don't, do you? Or else I'd be in the station already."

"You sure you want to do this with all these people around?"

"Why not? I don't have anything to hide." I grinned at the others in the waiting area. A few ducked their heads to avoid my gaze. I probably looked like some kind of maniac. And wasn't I? Mad with grief, they called it. Very Shakespearian.

"Huh. Nothing to hide when you're connected to three murders?"

"Four," I said automatically. *Shit, wait, they don't know I was there for Ferri's.* "You're forgetting this one," I added. "And last time I checked, I couldn't be in two places at once. Can't shoot a man from a distance if you're right next to him, can you?"

Harlow sneered. "Maybe *you* can't be in two places at once, but you can have an accomplice. And we think you and your friend were playing a little game of tag."

With a flourish he pulled papers out of his pocket. I nearly choked when I saw what they were: all the half-finished, ink-stained letters on Martin's desk. All of which matched the handwriting of the letters Emma had given to the police. I cursed myself. I should have run in to grab them before the ambulance got to the house. The letters plus the rifle plus the money I'd handed him from Emma... I could see why Harlow would think Martin and I looked very guilty, especially since he had been my alibi the night Taggart was killed.

"Coming now, Dawson?" Harlow asked, his voice dripping with fake sweetness.

I might have rolled over if it was just me, but I would be damned if I'd let him pin anything on Martin. "No. Check his gun. You'll see the bullets don't match."

Harlow's eyes narrowed.

Good. I'm making him think for once in his life. "Come find me when you have something real," I snapped.

He harrumphed and stalked off, making sure to shove me on his way past. The crowd in the ward continued to gape. Well, at least I'd given them something else to think about for a while. I was about to tell them the show was over when I noticed a man in a white coat standing open-mouthed in the doorway to the back.

"Er, Mr. Dawson?" he croaked.

The world shrank to just him. "Yeah?"

"Please come with me."

I followed slowly, missing how time had seemed so sluggish before. Beyond the door stank of bleach and blood, just like Martin's kitchen, but the only things I could see were bolts and bolts of ugly green curtains. The doctor swung a right into a small room. An office, I guessed. There was a desk and some cabinets. Finer details didn't make it past my tunnel-vision. He gestured at a chair, but I was far too jittery to sit.

He said words at me, but I only caught the gist over the ringing in my ears. Very serious. Low survivability. Would try their best. Better to go home and get some sleep. They would call if there were changes.

I walked out dazed, my ears buzzing. I'd thought hearing it would bring closure, but it just made things more terrible. And worse, I was going to have to tell Pearl.

THE STAFF OF the Ostia flowed around me, an uncaring ocean. Instinct drove me to Sev's office. I knocked and waited restlessly, anxious to find comfort in his arms.

To my surprise, it was Bella who answered the door, rosary still in her hand. My mouth fell open. "What're you doing here?" I asked before I could stop myself.

She shrugged. "I hear things, so I came to make sure *la mia gattina* was fine."

Just the implication that Pearl might not be fine set my already-frayed nerves on edge, and I barged past Bella into the room. But I needn't have worried. Pearl sat, legs dangling, in one of the armchairs in front of Sev's desk with a colorful children's book spread across her lap and her new doll tucked beside her. Sev stood behind the chair, watching me with uncertain eyes.

"Hi, Mr. Dawson!" Pearl held up her book. "Mr. Sev is helping me read."

Sev shrugged and gave a half smile. "Trying to. She's almost better than I am. Bella is the one who brought it though." He glanced at Pearl, then back at me. "It's kept her occupied."

Pearl nodded and beamed, but her face fell as she looked at me. "Is Mr. Martin okay?" she asked.

I almost burst into tears right there. How was I going to do this? I looked to Sev, who looked back with pity. I turned to Bella. She shook her head. No help, then. I took a few tentative steps into the room. Pearl stared, her eyes growing every second.

"Pearl..." The words stuck. I cleared my throat, but they remained caught. Without them, I resorted to parroting what the doctor had said. "They're going to do their best, and call us later."

Pearl's unease became pure distress. I didn't know why I'd thought I could trick her with vague words. She jumped off the chair, knocking both book and doll to the floor. "That's not fair!" she cried. "He's a nice man!"

Bella hurried forward and tried to coax Pearl into her arms. "*Gattina—*"

"No! I want Mr. Martin!" She ran and somehow slipped past me into the bustle of the backstage. Bella pushed me out of the way to chase her.

I was about to protest, but Sev's arm slid around my waist. "It's all right," he whispered. "Bella will take care of her."

"But I should... I should..."

"You should sit down."

He steered me to the armchair opposite the one Pearl had been in. He hovered next to me like a mother hen for a moment, then offered his now almost-empty cigarette case. I took one and let him light it for me, but I found that with my shaky breathing, all it made me do was cough. I tamped it out in the ashtray on the desk.

Sev sighed. "Is there anything I can do?"

I shook my head. "Not unless you're a miracle worker."

He watched me in silence, his foot tapping on the hardwood. Then he walked around to the other side of the desk. I watched him as he opened a drawer. He put a handgun next to the ashtray. "I asked Bella to bring this. You need to be able to defend yourself."

I stared at it. While I'd handled a gun—I'd been taught how to disarm one as part of my very brief training to be Carlisle's bodyguard—I'd never shot one, and I'd certainly never owned one. What was the point, anyway? I'd been too late and too far away to save Donnie and

Martin. But then, what if next time the bastard came after Sev or even Pearl? What if I was close enough to do something about it? I slid the gun off the desk into my pants pocket. It was heavier than I expected.

Sev's shoulders relaxed. Maybe he'd thought I'd put up a fight about it. "Do you—"

"I just want to get some sleep."

He nodded and started for the door. I struggled to stand, exhaustion weighing me down along with the gun. We passed Bella on the way out, somehow still poised like royalty in the folding chair next to the restroom. Pearl was curled in her lap, sobbing. She patted the girl's hair and cooed things at her in Italian, but it didn't seem to be helping. When we walked by she looked up, coolly nodding. Then she turned back to Pearl, but not before I saw tears in her eyes.

Chapter Twenty-Two

AS MUCH AS I wanted to sleep, I couldn't. There was just too much running through my mind, not to mention the pain of my throbbing head and sore arm. After waking Sev for the third time with my tossing and turning, I gave up trying. I spent what was left of the night jotting down everything I could remember about the murders in the hopes that something would become clearer, but it didn't. There had to be a thread I was missing. Maybe seeing Mrs. Green would help.

In the morning, Sev begged to come with me uptown. For protection, he said. I reminded him that the only person who had wanted to hurt me had been Taggart, and now the old boxer was dead.

"Still, *caro*, you're sticking your nose into places where it shouldn't go. Enough of that and maybe someone decides you're too much trouble to leave alive."

"Whoever it is has had plenty of opportunity to kill me and they haven't," I answered. *But why? What makes me special?*

"The police, then," he insisted. "Yesterday was the, what? Fourth time they came looking for you? They'll keep coming. They're like bloodhounds. And Bella won't be able to get you out."

"And what are you going to do to stop them? Gonna stab a cop?"

He shook his head. "You're not being reasonable."

"Look, it's going to be strange enough when I turn up at Mrs. Green's door asking questions. How do you think she'd react if you were standing next to me? You don't exactly look like you belong on that side of town."

That seemed to get through to him. He sighed. "At least take the gun, then."

I glanced at my sock drawer where I'd buried it as soon as we'd gotten home. While I had taken it willingly, I now regretted it. The damn thing just made me feel so uncomfortable. Even the metallic smell of it made me nauseated.

"If I take it," I said, "do you promise to stay here and keep out of trouble?"

"I promise." As if that was the end of the discussion, he retrieved the gun and handed it to me. "Be careful. Always watch. Keep your back to walls."

"I was a bodyguard. I think I know how to keep a lookout for trouble."

"Don't take this badly, but you didn't do such a good job before."

I flushed as I tucked the gun into my jacket pocket. "Yeah, well... I'm making up for it now."

"I know, which is why I said be careful. Reckless isn't the same thing as brave." He adjusted my jacket so it laid flat, then raised a warning finger. "Come back by noon or I will call the army down. I give you my word."

The bit about the army was an exaggeration, but I didn't doubt he'd come looking for me, and I wasn't sure I wanted to know what he'd do if he got frantic enough. So I nodded, kissed him, and got out of there before I changed my mind.

I CAUGHT THE trolley up to the high-class neighborhood. Mrs. Green lived in a sprawling Victorian building with gingerbread trim not too far from the Carlisles' house. It sat across from a patch of grass by the river edge with a bench that could have styled itself a park if it had been more than a few yards wide. Old-fashioned and quaint, just the kind of place an old lady would live in.

A maid answered the door and asked me to state my business. I gave her my name and said I'd worked for Carlisle, hoping that made it sound like we'd been neighbors. Mrs. Green *did* know me, after all. The maid disappeared for a few minutes, then returned saying I should wait in the private parlor.

I'd been in the house a few times during formal dinners, but never in that particular room. I was glad of it. It was rather ugly and overdone in chintz and lace, like someone had stopped trying to redecorate sometime during the first Roosevelt's administration. It smelled of mothballs and mildew.

"Ah, Mr. Dawson!"

Mrs. Green walked into the room, the chain for her glasses swinging with each step. She flitted to a chair, or at least as well as an old lady could flit, and gestured at a threadbare settee across from her. I eased myself onto the edge, mindful of my weight and the gun making strange angles in the interior pocket of my jacket. The sofa creaked, but held.

I decided politeness was the best way to go. "Thank you, ma'am. How are you today?"

To my surprise, she scoffed. "Oh, do leave off the pleasantries, Mr. Dawson. They are very tiresome, and at my age, I hoard all the seconds I can. What can I do for you? Still harping on about Roy's death?"

She'd always been a bit of a nasty old buzzard, but her callousness seemed excessive. Maybe she was going senile. "He was shot, ma'am," I said. "That makes it murder. Which means there's a murderer."

"Murders are for the police to investigate. Are you a policeman?"

"No."

"Then why are you here?"

Maybe sympathy would work? "You know the other man who was killed that night was Donald Kemp, and he was better than a father to me. I can't rest until I see justice done."

She rolled her eyes. "Emma told me you write for the pulps. I should have expected trite drivel like that out of your mouth."

Christ, she's worse than Bella! "Mrs. Green, please. I just want to know if you saw anything odd. I went back to the Ostia and from where you were sitting you could have seen the killer on the catwalk."

Her smirking mouth took a sudden downturn. "No." She jingled her glasses chain. "Can't see a thing without these on, I'm afraid."

I blinked at her. Her glasses were for reading. I'd seen her swan her way through parties and dinners with no problem, the glasses draped around her neck the whole time.

"I understand," I said. No sense in showing my hand. "But is there anything else you remember?"

She shook her head. "I was rather preoccupied with Roy and Emma's tiff." She sighed. "That poor woman. Roy was no saint, as I'm sure you know."

"I... had my suspicions." *Come on, tell me something I can use!*

Her lips twisted into a grin. "Oh, you don't know the half of it. He was having an affair, you know. With a lady of the night."

I tried to look shocked. "I had no idea."

"I'm sure you had some. Mr. Kemp knew all about it. He played emissary so much he was practically the girl's pimp."

I swallowed the rage clawing at my throat over her insult to Donnie. "I'm sure it wasn't like that."

"Oh, wasn't it?" She leaned in, the wicked smile still on her face. She was proud to tell me these things, pleased to drag dead men's names through the mud. "Roy knew what he was doing. He borrowed from me to keep Emma from seeing money go missing. And when I cut him off, well! He didn't even slow down."

So, that was why Carlisle had resorted to gambling and racketeering. His money pot had dried up, and had probably been demanding interest.

"I think he went a bit mad in the end," Mrs. Green continued. "He came scraping for a few hundred more after I'd told him I was done, and he said he was going to marry the girl! Can you imagine? Divorce Emma and marry some trollop half his age!"

Divorce? Then he hadn't been lying to Birdie when he said he'd leave his wife. Had Emma known? If she had, would she have spilled half the tears she did?

"Did you give him the money?" I asked. "Do you know what he did with it?"

"I gave him two hundred to stop him from whining, but I never got a cent back. Presumably it didn't just go to the girl. I can't imagine she was that expensive."

Two hundred, the same amount Harlow had found at Donnie's place. I had assumed it was for more gambling, or for Birdie, but Mrs. Green was right—that was a considerable sum for either of those things. Maybe it had been seed money for a new life? But Carlisle had just announced his election bid. He wouldn't have done that if he had been planning on running off. While it could have been a ruse to keep Emma in the dark as long as possible, I doubted it. Carlisle simply hadn't been that bright.

But if he was so dim, maybe he'd thought he *could* get away with just tossing Emma to the side with no repercussions to his political career. Two hundred could buy the services of one hell of a divorce lawyer. Even with Carlisle's infidelity, a good lawyer could spin anything. And as Sev had learned, in a court of law, it wasn't so much the truth as it was the public's opinion. If Carlisle had gotten the jump on Emma, he could have made her look like an overbearing shrew, at the very least. Bonus, he could have used the publicity to his advantage in the election. Sympathy could go a long way.

"Why did you lend Carlisle so much money if you knew what he was doing?" I asked.

"Surely, you do not deny your neighbors and friends when they ask for help?" Mrs. Green answered with a fabricated smile.

I felt nauseated. And worried. "Can I ask why you're telling me this?"

She laughed and twisted the chain around her finger. "Roy is dead, which means I won't see that money again unless someone else knows about it. You are still in Emma's good graces. You could get her to return the money, I'm sure." She winked, clearly still under the impression that Emma and I were about to start something if we hadn't already.

That took bravery, asking a woman to pay back the money her dead husband had borrowed in order to divorce her. "Ma'am, I don't want to be anyone's messenger." I rubbed my arm. It still hurt. "People kill them too often. Can't you...invite her to tea or something and talk about it?"

"Don't be uncouth. One does not discuss finances over tea. This is not a difficult job, Mr. Dawson. I'm sure even someone with your limited skills can manage it."

"What if I refuse?" She wouldn't have asked if she didn't think she had some kind of hold over me. Not that I had anything to use as leverage. No job, no friends. About to lose my apartment. Cops already on my tail. And to be frank, with Sev already outed, our relationship wasn't going to be a secret much longer.

"Well, I can't force you, no, but I think you may want to do it to keep your friend Mr. Kemp's name clean. Wouldn't you rather me handle this quietly than sue for it and have all this dirty laundry come out?"

I hesitated. While borrowing the money wasn't illegal, using it to pay a prostitute and gamble were. Carlisle had been careful about not handling the money himself. It had all gone through Donnie. And while someone was digging after that, they might find any number of other things. Not that Donnie could be put in prison, but I couldn't bring myself to sully his memory for something so stupid as refusing to ask Emma Carlisle to fork over some cash she probably wouldn't even miss in the end.

But still, I couldn't meet Mrs. Green's eyes when I agreed. "What do you want me to tell her?"

"Whatever you see fit," she answered. "Emma will want to turn the whole thing over to her father. Which will be fine. Accountants can't be trusted, you know. Always nosing around when the numbers don't match. They're almost like little boys playing detective."

I ignored the dig. "That's all, right? Just tell her?"

"Yes, unless you'd like to add something else. No? No, I didn't think so. Don't fret so much. It will sound nicer coming from you. You have a sad face. Contrite. She'll listen to you." Mrs. Green reached over and rang a bell. "But do smile a little. You're going down the street, not to the gallows. I would advise some acting lessons if you wish to continue working at this level of society. It doesn't do to be read like a book." The maid appeared in the doorway. Mrs. Green folded her hands in her lap. "See Mr. Dawson out. He is a very busy man."

Sometime during my visit with Mrs. Green the weather had turned heavy and damp, threatening rain. I was almost glad. Sunlight didn't quite match my mood. I cursed myself the whole half block it took to get to the Carlisles' house. Suckered by an old lady, I couldn't believe it! Well, I could, considering the amount of corruption in town. Everyone with their money and their secrets. I was almost surprised no one I knew had been murdered before.

I knocked on the door, and it was opened by the same girl who had let me in a few days ago. She smiled at me but seemed confused.

"May I speak to Mrs. Carlisle?" I asked.

She hesitated, but just at that moment, Emma was walking past the foyer door. She saw me and exclaimed, "Alex! What a pleasant surprise."

I tugged on the cuff of my borrowed jacket, hoping she wouldn't ask about their ill-fit or the revolver-shaped bulge near my chest. "Mrs. Carlisle, I've just come from seeing Mrs. Green."

"Mrs. Green?" Emma's plucked eyebrows rose almost to her hairline. "Whatever did she want from you?"

"Is there somewhere we could talk?"

"Oh, of course!"

She led me into the parlor again. The stupid stuffed fox leered at me like I was an unwelcome guest. Considering what I was about to say, I probably was.

"Just wait here, Alex. I'll get my father. We were just about to have tea."

"I don't think—"

But she was already calling out the door. "Papa! Mr. Dawson is here."

The floorboards creaked in objection to the mass that was Marc Logan walking across them. He took up almost the entirety of the doorway when he came in. His reaction upon seeing me was to squint and scowl. I might have thought he was unhappy at my presence, but he looked like that all the time. Somebody had told me once that he hadn't smiled since his wife died, but I knew that wasn't true. I had seen him smile at Emma a number of times. He nodded once as he towered opposite me. "Dawson."

"Mr. Logan, sir." I could feel my heartbeat in my neck. Telling Emma anything had just become more difficult.

But she didn't seem to notice my anxiety as she flopped onto the settee. "Now, what is it you wanted to tell me?"

She didn't faint when I told her, thank God. She blinked, like she didn't understand what I'd said to her. She turned to her father, but he didn't change his expression. He did, however, take a step forward.

"I think you should go," he said quietly.

I couldn't disagree. I nodded my goodbyes as Emma continued to look dismayed and lost. But as I was seeing myself out, I remembered the suspicious letter I had borrowed from her. Was it even relevant? After all, I'd only identified who'd written the ones that had come to Rutherford and the *Journal*, not hers. But connection was connection, right? And the content of the letter had been threats against Carlisle and his supposed corruption, which everyone now knew was true. It wasn't like I was telling her lies. But I couldn't imagine Emma would ever want to hear another word out of my mouth.

"Mr. Dawson? Alex?"

I turned away from the door at Emma's voice. She was standing in the entrance to the hall. "Yes, ma'am?"

"Thank you. For coming here and telling me. It was very brave."

"I don't know about brave..."

"But it was!" She stepped into the vestibule. "Especially in front of my father. He loved Roy like he was his own son. To hear this..."

"Um, where is Mr. Logan?" I expected him to lunge out of the parlor to haul me away to have a stern talking to at the least. Not that I needed to be threatened to keep quiet. I'd had enough. As soon as I put Donnie's ghost to bed, I was getting out of town.

"He's gone upstairs to lie down. I'm afraid this has rather rattled him. And at his age..." She came closer to me, close enough that she could touch me if she reached out. "Please don't blame yourself. I'm glad it was you who told us. I don't think I could have borne it if someone else had."

What could I say to that? That it had been my pleasure? "Well, it was Mr. Kemp who helped him, and I... It's my responsibility now."

She took another step closer. Did she just have no perception of personal space? I edged away, annoyed. I'd heard some people got amorous in the face of grief, but as far as I knew, I'd never led her on, and she'd never shown any interest before, so her behavior struck me as bizarre. But now that she was here alone without Logan looming over us, I could ask some harder-hitting questions.

"I'm going to ask you something, Mrs. Carlisle, and I know it's going to sound strange, but–"

"I was not unfaithful to Roy. And I don't think he was going to leave me. He may have looked, but men always look, don't they?"

"I couldn't say one way or the other." I cleared my throat. "But that's not what I was going to ask about. The letter you gave me before. Do you know who sent it? It wasn't the same person as sent the others."

Her brow furrowed. "No? How do you know?"

"I've got a friend in the newspaper business. One of the old ones had been dropped off at the *Journal*. I brought yours to them and the handwriting didn't match. The style didn't either."

"I see." She pursed her lips. "Well, the plot thickens, then, doesn't it?"

I was tempted to tell her that it had thinned a whole hell of a lot now that Bella Bellissima was a ghost of herself and Martin was dying in some green-curtained hell, but screaming incomprehensible things at rich young women was a one-way ticket to the loony bin.

"Oh, goodness, what happened to your arm?" Emma asked. Her thin, ivory fingers pattered on the cuff and the bandages underneath.

I yanked my arm back. What right did she have to touch me? "Got scraped up the other night."

Emma looked at me through her eyelashes and pouted. "Do be careful, Alex. Whatever would we do if you were taken from us too?"

"I'm sure you'd figure out something." I took another step away from her. "Now, I hate to run when you obviously want to talk things out, but I've got someone waiting on me."

"Oh yes, I'm sorry to have kept you." She backed away, like it had just now occurred to her that maybe it was a bad idea to be that close.

I bolted, my head buzzing with every terrible thing that had happened in the last two weeks. Carlisle was corrupt as any big-time politician. Emma was a flirt, if not an outright cheat. Even a little old lady like Mrs. Green was feeding into the problem. And Donnie had helped. Maybe Vern had been right about how everyone had a skeleton in their closet, and maybe he was right about using them to his advantage too. I had tried to be kind and careful and all it had gotten me was a bunch of lies and obfuscations.

I saw the trolley slog its way up the hill and ran for it. It was well before noon and I could have waited for the next one, but I was desperate to go home. Besides, the clouds were darkening, and it was only a matter of time before it started to pour. I hopped on board just as the first fat drops splattered into the street. The trolley lurched forward, and I stared out the window at the huge houses.

Something white and orange flickered from one shrubbery to another, catching my eye. Just a cat. No, not any cat. That was Pearl's cat Daisy; I was almost sure of it. But what was the damn animal doing so far away from the neighborhood? The last I had seen of it had been when it ran from Martin's yard. For half a second, I thought about pulling the chain to get off at the next stop but reconsidered. Not only would it be very silly to go chasing a cat I wasn't even sure was Pearl's, but if I caught the stupid thing, I'd have had to hold it in place until the next trolley came around, and I had no intention of doing that. Especially with my arm already cut to ribbons.

The trolley picked up speed as it coasted down the hill, and I lost sight of even the bushes. I slumped back on the bench. What did a dumb cat matter in the scheme of things anyway?

Chapter Twenty-Three

BY THE TIME the trolley reached my stop, the rain was coming down hard. The already-sagging houses seemed to wilt even more under the weight of the storm. What was left of the sidewalk stood as cement islands on gravel that had turned to mud. I hunched my shoulders and pulled down my hat. What was some water compared to everything else?

I didn't see Vern until I almost walked into him. I looked up, startled.

"Come on, Dawson, pull yourself together." He stretched his arm all the way up so his umbrella could cover my head as well as his. "You're gonna catch a cold or something. What the hell are you doing out in this storm?"

"Going home. What are *you* doing?"

"Going to see you! Phones are funny because of the rain." His expression turned more serious. "The coroner let out the report on John Rutherford this morning. Died of liver atrophy."

I blinked at him. "What does that even mean?"

"I dunno. But they say it was probably caused by an overdose of ch..." He scrambled in his breast pocket for his own notebook. "Chincophen," he garbled out. "Gout medication."

"That doesn't make any sense," I said. "I was there earlier that day. He said he was very careful about his medication."

"Maybe he got confused. He was old, losing it, maybe."

"He was *definitely* not confused when I saw him." A chill ran down my spine. Something was very, very off.

"But that wasn't the only thing I wanted to see you about," Vern continued. He lowered his voice. "I heard what happened yesterday to your friend. Is—"

Just what I didn't need, emotional whiplash. I'd successfully managed to keep thoughts of Martin at bay the whole morning, but here they were again at a word. "I don't want to talk about it."

That might have put someone else off, but not Vern. If there was one adjective to describe him, it was persistent. "What did the police say about it?"

"They think Martin killed Carlisle and Donnie, and together we offed Taggart and then I killed him to keep him quiet. They were bothering me about it already."

Vern's brow furrowed. "Now that's just stupid. Kill someone? You? Punch them, sure, but kill?" He shook his head. "And I don't know the other guy, but—"

"Martin is a good man," I said.

He nodded. "I'm sure he is if you're his friend."

The rain pattered loudly in the awkward silence. Water leaked into my shoes and soaked into my socks, making me shiver. Vern grunted and shoved the umbrella into my hand.

"Take it. I'll get a cab back to the office."

"You sure?" I asked, surprised.

"Yes. Just bring it around with you next time." He clapped his hand on my elbow. "Be smart. I don't want to be writing about you." He started to leave. "I'll keep an ear open. Let you know if I hear anything else."

"Thanks."

He got a few yards away before he turned back. "Oh, and I've been hearing some other things," he called. "About you and a mutual friend of ours." He traced a line down his cheek in the same place Sev's scar was.

I shrugged. "They're true."

"Huh. Didn't think it'd become a thing." He jammed his hands in his pockets and curled in on himself to avoid the rain. "At least something's going right, right?"

SEV WAS LOUNGING on the bed with a book in his hand when I came in. He sat up and grinned. "See? I was well behaved. And look what I found." He held up the book. I realized it was my author copy of the dime romance I'd put out last year. "You wrote this?"

"Yeah." *Ugh, don't remind me.* "Well, most of it." I shook out the umbrella and dumped it in the corner, then hurried to the dresser and stuffed the gun under several pairs of darned socks. Without it I felt ten pounds lighter. "Why? That bad?"

"No, it's very good." He smirked. "But maybe I'm partial."

"At least it didn't run you off."

"It would take a lot more than bad writing to run me off." He kept smiling, his gold eyes searching my face for a positive reaction, but it faded when he didn't find it. "What happened, Alex? She didn't know anything?"

"Worse." I crossed the room and slumped next to him, letting his warmth seep through my soaked clothes. "She knows something, but she won't tell. *And* she's a filthy extortionist."

I told him the whole story, and at the end he tutted his disappointment. "And I thought my family had problems."

I remembered Bella's punishment. I put my hand on his cheek. The ridge of the scar felt smooth among the stubble. "Did you want to try talking to your mom at all?"

He patted my hand. "No. I think I'm done fighting battles with her." The crow's feet appeared at the corners of his eyes. "Besides, I've got you. As long as one of us learns to cook, we should be fine."

At the mention of cooking, my stomach growled. The aching pit in my core wasn't just from frustration. I hadn't eaten breakfast and yesterday's dinner had only been picked at. And I hadn't eaten anything since the dinner before *that*...

Sev must have done the calculations too because his face grew concerned. "You know what you need, *caro*? A solid meal and some rest. Why don't you take a nap, and I'll find us some food." He stood, leaving the space beside me cold and empty. "I'll get some sandwiches."

"Can you sneak in and out okay?" I asked.

"I did it before. And if I get caught..." He produced the knife from his pocket and slipped it back in. "I know what I'm doing."

I made a face. Even Sev joking about more violence was off-putting. But I doubted he'd get caught at all, let alone be forced to cut someone up. My imagination was just running wild between the lack of food and sleep and all the other nonsense going on.

"Go to sleep," he insisted as he snatched up the umbrella. "I'll be back in twenty minutes."

That was as good a plan as any, so I stripped off my drenched tie, jacket, and shoes so I could lay down while he was gone. The space where he'd been was comfortably warm, and I curled into it. I didn't expect to sleep—my whole body felt like it was being twisted and set on fire—

but I must have at least dozed because the next thing I knew someone was knocking on the door.

"Wha'd you do? Lock yourself out?" I mumbled as I groped my way from the bed.

Mr. Blake stood in the hall. "Phone call for you," he murmured. "City hospit–"

I shoved past him and ran down the stairs, my socked feet sliding on the floorboards. *No no no no Christ no...*

I knew what the doctor was going to tell me before he said it. Hell, I'd known the second I heard Pearl scream for help. But that didn't stop my heart from hammering so loudly that the words were almost lost in my ears. He was, of course, very sorry for my loss. Then he asked me politely, gently, what the arrangements should be, and I found myself rattled. Even the money Emma had given me was gone, into Harlow's custody if not his pocket. I stammered something about needing to get back to him before hanging up. Or trying to hang up. My hands were shaking so much I missed on the first go.

The world felt... I didn't have the word. Hollow? Empty? With both Donnie and Martin gone, I was without guidance for the first time in almost a decade. Alone.

I wandered back up the stairs, only half seeing due to tears in my eyes, and flopped into my bed, not even bothering to shut the door. Sev found me sobbing a few minutes later. He didn't ask what was the matter, he didn't need to. He just shut the door, dropped the bag of sandwiches on my desk, and wrapped his arms around me. It felt like ages, but it wasn't long before I cried myself out. I didn't even the energy for tears.

"We should tell Pearl," I croaked, peeling myself out of Sev's embrace.

"It can wait. Or I'll ask Bella to tell her."

"No, it needs to be me. And it needs to be now. Before I lose my nerve."

He sighed and shook his head. "All right. Get your shoes and meet me by the payphone. I'll call Bella to let her know we're coming."

AFTER HE FINISHED talking to Bella, Sev hailed us a cab. I didn't know the address he gave the driver and didn't bother to ask where we were going. My head felt like it was stuffed with cotton, making all my thoughts slow. The cab dropped us at an intersection I didn't recognize. Sev walked some, then ducked into an alley. I followed, hardly aware of the rain still cascading down.

The building he stopped at was nondescript, cement and windowless, tucked among dozens like it. Perhaps it had was a storehouse of some sort? Sev knocked on the steel door, and it echoed back in a dull baritone. A few seconds later, some heavy lock I couldn't see was undone with a clunk. Bella's wolfish guard swung open the door. He squinted at me. Maybe I should have felt threatened, but I was numb, my blood still boiling in my ears. If he wanted to kill me, well, I was in no condition to stop him. But he let us in without a word.

A metal staircase spiraled down to unknown depths, but we walked past it into a dingy hall with a string of single bulbs giving off inadequate light. Even in my haze, the pattern on the wall struck me as peculiar: black, uneven marks on the cream paint, some almost as high as my head. I touched one of the stains. Ash and grit. Fire damage? Why would we be somewhere that had been burned out?

The decrepit nature of the place didn't seem to bother Sev or the guard. They kept walking until they came to the door at the other end of the hall. It was the industrial sort with rivets holding iron to iron. Instinct told me that whatever was behind it was dangerous. Sensing my unease, Sev squeezed my hand.

The guard opened the door and to my surprise, it wasn't another soot-blackened room, but a space that could only be described as flowery. Four or five baskets of chrysanthemums and calla lilies were clustered on top of and around a heavily carved coffee table. Behind them was a desk with gilded brackets and sparkling paperweights holding court on the blotter. A floor lamp next to it had stained-glass wisteria for a shade. Striped and floral wallpaper covered the walls in a dizzying pattern. Its egregious opulence reminded me of nothing so much as the Ostia.

This has to be Bella's office.

Almost like she could read my mind, she stepped into view, starkly plain in her black dress against her gaudy surroundings. "Well, come in," she snapped.

Sev nudged me forward, and I crept into the room. It was even bigger than it had looked from the outside, the remaining space taken up by parlor furniture including a full china cabinet of blue delftware. Pearl wasn't anywhere to be seen.

"Where's Pearl?" I asked.

"She will not come out to speak to me." Bella indicated a less-impressive door on the far wall, then crossed her arms over her chest. "But before you let her know you are here, I wanted to say..." She paused like it pained her. "I wanted to say you were right. In your note. Romano was the one who betrayed us."

It took a few seconds to realize that she meant the third guard at the diner, the one who had been murdered along with Ferri. "Oh. Did you find out who he told?"

"No, but we will." She scowled. "Romano is lucky that they were the one who killed him. I would not have been so clean about it."

Out of the corner of my eye, I caught Sev wincing. Whatever he was thinking, I didn't want to know.

Bella stepped away and knocked on the door she'd indicated. "*Gattina*," she called, "Mr. Dawson is here to see you."

There was a pause, then Pearl eased it open a crack. "Hi."

"Hi," I said. "Can I come talk to you?"

She glanced at the others in the room. "Just you?"

"Yeah, just me."

She nodded and moved away, leaving the door open. I hesitated before following, but it was something I had to do.

The other room turned out to be a walk-in closet, though it was packed with dresses and accessories worth more than my whole block. Pearl sat in the middle of the floor and danced her doll across her knee. She had a new dress, but it had far too much out-of-fashion lace to have been recently bought. Had it belonged to Bella's daughter? I wiped the thought out of my mind.

I knelt in front of her. "Pearl," I whispered so my breath wouldn't hitch, "Martin died this afternoon."

She raised her head and regarded me in silence.

Kids are smart. They always know. "You figured, didn't you?" I said. "After what I said yesterday."

She nodded, and as she did her face contorted, and tears welled in her eyes. She jumped up and latched on to me. She cried without making a sound, no doubt a side-effect of years of ill-treatment. I let her stay in my arms until she slid onto the floor, exhausted and hiccupping. I wished I had something more useful to say or do, but I was at a loss. If only Martin... No, there was no Martin anymore. No Donnie. Just me. I was the one who had to fix it now.

I searched for something that I could distract her with, but the only thing I saw that a child might like was her own toy. "Say," I said with a mock-cheerful tone, "that's a pretty doll. Does she have a name?"

Pearl snuffled before answering. "Nancy."

"Did Bella give her to you?"

She shook her head. "Miss Bella didn't give her to me."

Not Bella? "Then who?"

"The other pretty lady."

I rocked back on my heels, confusion shouldering its way in with my other emotions. What the hell was she talking about? Maybe she was just mixed up, thinking Bella in her jewelry and furs was a different person than Bella in mourning. I knew I felt muddled enough that I might have made that kind of error, and I wasn't six years old. Hell, maybe Bella had a maid I hadn't run into yet.

"Well, you be sure to thank her, all right?"

Pearl nodded.

I stood and helped her to her feet. "Do you like staying with Bella?"

She shrugged. "She's okay. I miss Mr. Martin."

"Yeah, me too."

Bella gladly took custody of Pearl again once I led her out of the closet, and before I could say anything, the wolfish guard hustled Sev and I toward the exit.

"No! I wanted to go with him!" Pearl shouted.

It almost shattered my heart, but no, she *had* to go with Bella. I couldn't hide both her and Sev in my single room, a room that I was about a week from losing because I couldn't make rent.

"It's better if you stay with Miss Bella," I insisted. "And it's not like I'm going away forever."

That didn't persuade her, and Pearl dissolved into a full-fledged tantrum, shrieking and tugging on Bella's skirts. I had to hurry away so I wouldn't cry with her. The guard slammed the door shut after us, but I could still hear her screaming through it. I slumped against the wall and struggled to breathe evenly.

"*Caro.*" Sev took my hand. "It'll be all right."

My rage flared for half a second. How could it be all right after everything that had happened? But then I saw his eyes, brown in the dim light of the burned hallway, and I knew I had to be brave. For everyone's sakes.

Chapter Twenty-Four

I SPENT THE rest of the afternoon in a stupor. I ate the sandwich and dozed and woke back up and paced the apartment. When I got sick of moving, I sat at my desk and wrote out everything I'd learned at Mrs. Green's. For a long time, I stared at my own notes about the murders, hoping something would jump out at me. Sev watched me, foot tapping, but didn't interfere. Maybe I'd made him edgy, or maybe he was just as lost as I was. Eventually he gave up and went to bed. I continued poring through my notebook.

A clatter made me jump, but I decided to ignore it. Vermin knocking things around was the least of my problems. Then it happened again.

I turned, searching for the noise. Sev was asleep, his arms tucked under his pillow, nowhere near the nightstand. Nothing looked like it had fallen of its own accord. Maybe a neighbor? I glanced at my clock. It was well past eleven. Who else in the building would be up at this hour?

The sound happened once more. The window. My stomach knotted. Ferri had been shot through a window, after all.

I nudged the curtains open. The rain had stopped, and standing under the streetlamp was Vern with a handful of gravel. He waved at me. My stomach plunged again, and I hurried downstairs.

"I couldn't get in," Vern snapped as I jammed the romance paperback into the front door so it wouldn't shut and lock me out, "and the phones are still out—"

"What happened?" I panted. The damp ground felt cold and gritty under my bare feet.

Vern's face was ashen in the weak light of the streetlamp. "You know Mrs. Green? The Carlisles' neighbor?"

"Yeah, I talked to her earlier today. What about her?"

"She was found smothered to death in her own living room."

"What! When?"

"A few hours ago, maybe? I don't know, I just heard about it myself."

The world froze. Like Rutherford, she turned up dead less than twelve hours after having spoken to me. Harlow was going to have a field day if he found out. But that couldn't just be bad luck on my part. Someone was killing the people I talked to. I needed my notebook. I needed to see all the pieces in one place.

"Where are you going?" Vern demanded.

I waved him away as I mounted the first step of the stoop. "I have to think."

"Think? Dawson, you need to *leave!*" he exclaimed. "I'm not even sure the cops will wait until morning to come get you."

I whirled to face him. "I told you already, I'm not leaving this city until I figure this out. Donnie would never forgive me if I did."

I left Vern protesting as I rushed back to my room. Sev flinched awake as the door slammed. He blinked at me and mumbled something in Italian.

"It's fine," I said. "Go back to sleep."

He grunted and sank back down.

For what must have been the hundredth time, I traced my finger under the bullet points I'd written. Carlisle and Donnie shot from the catwalk at the Ostia. Mrs. Green should have been able to see something. I scribbled in another sentence in the margin about how she must have, but had refused to speak about it, and instead chose to lean on Logan and Emma for money. Under that I'd written how Bella's third guard, the one named Romano, had betrayed her and had probably been the person to let the murderer in or at least sneak in the rifle, since I was sure no one could have just waltzed into the Ostia with a weapon that obvious.

Donnie had been given money by Carlisle to pass into unsavory hands, whether it was for prostitution or gambling. Or a divorce lawyer, I'd scrawled. As for why, I assumed Donnie's good nature had gotten the better of him, but it was also possible that he'd been blackmailed into it. Just because I hadn't known about his past didn't mean Carlisle hadn't. In any case, some of the money had ended up with Taggart, who was later killed in almost the same way. For some reason, someone thought I also had dirty money and called the cops on me.

Someone had taken a shot at Bella, missed, then tried again, this time succeeding in killing her husband. The murderer had also taken out Romano for good measure, presumably to ensure Bella couldn't torture him into telling who he had worked with. Mrs. Green had known about the money and the affair, and had no problem squeezing people to get what she wanted. John Rutherford had somehow overdosed on pills he was well-aware could kill him.

But how did Martin fit in? Had it been about the letters? Who had brought the one to the newspaper, and who had written the other? Who had even known Martin wrote them besides me, and then Vern when I told him? The police hadn't even figured it out until they rummaged through his house.

Could the connection be the gun? But Martin hadn't even kept the damn thing loaded. He'd hated the war, hid all evidence of his involvement, unlike Logan who proudly displayed his uniform in his office.

His office. Where Emma had gotten the last letter, the one Martin hadn't written. Logan knew all about the ones that had come to Carlisle and could have forged his own.

Everything tumbled into place. Logan had already been at the Ostia, only the gun had needed to be smuggled in. Considering Bella's troop of criminals, it would have been simple and unremarkable if Romano had just walked in with it. I hadn't seen Logan at the table when I turned to see Carlisle and Donnie dead, only Emma. In fact, I couldn't remember seeing him at all until several minutes later.

While I couldn't guarantee Logan had been at the church or the diner, I couldn't guarantee that he hadn't either. Same for Taggart. Same for Martin, who like Romano, had known too much, though Martin hadn't known he'd had crucial information. Rutherford had last been seen at Carlisle's memorial service. He could easily have eaten or drunk something Logan handed him, and it would have been easy for a man Logan's size to hold a pillow down on an old woman until she stopped breathing.

But why?

Because he'd somehow figured out Carlisle was going to leave Emma. Scandal. Shame. Not to mention losing the house and the money. When faced with losing everything, some men just let it happen and mourned, but some men did something about it, and Logan was definitely one of the latter.

I should be one of those people.

It was stupid and dangerous, but there were so many people who'd died, so many whose lives had been mangled. It wasn't just about justice for Donnie anymore. It was justice for Martin, justice for Pearl and Sev and me.

I grabbed my shoes and jacket and a handful of change for a cab since the trolleys didn't run so late. I fished the gun out of the drawer and slid it into my pocket. It still felt heavy, but it didn't make me cringe like it had when I'd first hidden it. Now, it gave me a giddy kind of strength. I was going to stop this. Hell, maybe afterward I'd walk right into the station house and turn myself in to Harlow.

I pressed my hands against the glass of the window, squinting to make sure Vern had gone. He had, and I prepared to leave. Then I heard the bed squeak as Sev shifted onto his side. I stared at him for a moment. His hair was mussed, the curls sticking up at random. I smiled despite myself. He was the one good thing to come out of all of this. He didn't deserve to be abandoned.

I ripped paper out of my notebook and wrote everything about the murders that I could think of, both the facts and my conclusions. The second page contained everything else, my reasons for what I was going to do and my apologies. I was going to leave it on the desk, but I thought it might get lost, or that Harlow would get his grubby paws on it before Sev could, so I laid it on my pillow instead. Sev sighed in his sleep.

I'd written it, but I had to say it in case I didn't get the chance again. "Hey, Sev," I whispered next to his ear, "I love you."

The corner of his mouth curved slightly upward, but otherwise he didn't respond. I wasn't even sure he'd heard me. But there wasn't time, and I didn't want to wake him in case he tried to stop me.

Chapter Twenty-Five

I HAD THE cab leave me at the bottom of the hill just in case someone saw it and became suspicious. It took a while to hike up the incline, and even longer for someone to come to the door. I wasn't sure if the maid ran off to get Logan because she believed my story about knowing vital information about Carlisle's death or because she didn't want to cross a man who looked like he'd walked through hell.

The floorboards announced Logan's approach. Even in slippers and a dressing gown, he was imposing, taking up most of the space of the doorway. But a bullet in the right place, and even the biggest man would go down.

"Mr. Dawson," he said as flatly as he'd ever said it. "What can I do for you? It is quite late, as I'm sure you're aware."

I'd stormed in wanting to kill him, and now that he was in front of me... I couldn't just shoot him in his own foyer, could I? With Emma and the maid God-knew-where in the house? I needed to buy myself a moment to think.

"I... I heard Mrs. Green was killed today," I said.

He nodded. "Yes. It will probably be in the papers in the morning."

"Is there anything you'd like to tell me that the papers wouldn't know about?"

His eyes narrowed. "No."

"Is... is there anything you'd like to tell me about the night Mr. Carlisle was killed?"

"No." He began to turn away. "Now, if you'll excuse me, Mr. Dawson, I–"

I pulled out the gun. "Mr. Logan, wait."

He turned back. He looked at my face, then the gun. His lips thinned, but that was his only reaction.

I tried to keep my hands from shaking. "How about you come with me?"

His expression didn't change. "Yes, I think that's best."

He walked past me and took his hat and coat off the stand in the hall. I couldn't tell if he was scared or not. I knew I was terrified. What was I doing with a gun trained on Marc Logan? Why had I even thought this was a good idea at all? But if I put it away and begged for forgiveness I'd never know what really happened. And then he would probably have me arrested on top of everything else. The decision had been made, and it was too late to change.

Logan and I went to the small park at the end of the street, across from Mrs. Green's house. I didn't keep the gun aimed at him, but he didn't try to run or take it from me. Even being threatened, he was as cold and calm as a sheet of ice.

I indicated a bench near the river. "Sit."

He did as I asked and even leaned back. "You wanted to ask me something?"

I swallowed. Christ, what was I doing? But this was the chance to get answers. I leveled the pistol at his chest. I kept my finger off the trigger, though, in case my trembling fingers got the better of me. "Did you kill Roy Carlisle?"

His blue eyes stared into mine. "Yes."

I was shocked. I hadn't been expecting him to answer at all, let alone in the positive. "Did... did you kill Bert Taggart too?" I stammered.

He continued to watch me with cold eyes. "Who is Bert Taggart?"

"The boxing guy Carlisle bribed."

"Oh, yes, little Pearl's father. Yes, I did."

"And Martin? Mrs. Green?"

"Yes."

Blood rushed in my ears. "And... and were you the one taking shots at Bella Bellissima?"

"Yes. Though I am ashamed to say I missed twice." The corner of Logan's lips turned up. Not quite a smile, but an indication he was pleased with himself. "I was a marksman in the war. Did your friend Martin never tell you that?"

"Well, what about Rutherford?"

"I'm surprised you caught that. Yes. Stuffs his face like a pig. It wasn't hard to hide pills in his food—"

"But why would you kill them?" It came out as more of a whine than a question. "Couldn't you have just killed Carlisle and let that be the end?"

Logan's eyes lit up. "But he was just the tip of everything, wasn't he? He was a symptom of a cancer. The corruption did not begin with him and it will not end with him."

"So this was some kind of moral crusade?" I gaped at him. "You're a lunatic, a goddamn lunatic..."

"Not as much of one as your doctor friend. He was the one writing those letters, you know."

"You leave Martin out of this," I said through clenched teeth. "He's innocent, and you framed him! You brought the letter to the *Journal* so someone would make the connection even if the police didn't."

"He is an anarchist, and he deserves what he got."

"No, he didn't! Donnie didn't either! They were just good men who got caught up in something. Like..." I glanced at the gun in my hand. *Like me.*

Logan stood up. He towered over me. "I do not hurt the innocent, Mr. Dawson. I only want justice and the safety of this city. Put the gun down, son. You haven't done anything yet."

I hovered there, unsure. No, I hadn't done anything yet, at least not to Logan. If I ran right then, I could probably get away. Grab Sev, start a new life. Pearl could stay with Bella. Vern could write whatever he wanted. Everyone else could go to hell. And yet my feet stayed planted on the soggy grass.

There was a gunshot. I yelped as Logan's forehead burst into a small geyser of blood and pulp. He swayed for a second, half headless, then crumbled. I stared at his body, then at the gun in my hand. It hadn't gone off.

"A pity Papa always believed that honesty is the best policy."

I recognized the voice and spun. Emma approached from the direction of the house wearing little more than a trench coat thrown over a silk nightdress. She spread her hands out. In one, she held a smoking revolver.

"Why would you do that?" I sputtered.

"Because you wouldn't have, coward that you are." Emma strolled up next to the bench. She looked down at her father's body and made a face. "Disgusting. I shouldn't have aimed for the head. But then, that's what he always did."

I raised my pistol, but my hands were shaking so much that I was aiming at nothing. "Tell me what's going on!"

She rolled her eyes. "Have you ever even shot a gun?"

"I–"

She ignored me and kept going. "You and your pathetic little one-man investigation. You're so attached to that man. What was his name? Donald? Don't tell me you were sleeping with him before your new little fairy friend?"

I struggled to breathe as my throat closed up. "Don't you dare bring Sev into this! How do you even know about him?"

"You may be familiar with a little girl. Large eyes, fondness for cats. Father was a drunk. Like yours, I hear. Seems she needed a place to go when she couldn't stay with her doctor friend anymore and Miss Bellissima let her fend for herself. Nor could she stay with you because you preferred to keep your den of pleasure to yourself. Pearl was *so* happy to tell me all your little secrets, especially when I gave her that doll."

"The pretty lady was you, not Bella," I whispered. That explained Daisy being up there. It was probably the last place the stupid cat had gotten anything reasonable to eat.

"Miss Bellissima thinks she owns this town. I can't wait to assure her that she does not." Emma shook her head. "I can't believe he missed her twice."

"You...you knew about the murders?"

"Of course I knew. All it took was a little nudge. Poor Papa could never say no to me."

"...Nudge?"

Emma laughed. Its cultured, tinkling sound was unsuited to the situation. "All I had to do was make suggestions. Though Mr. Rutherford was Papa's idea. But he isn't much good at stealth, so I had to step in." She mimed sprinkling something, then waved her hand. "The only one he refused to do was you. He kept saying you were an innocent man, even after he found out about your...deviant tendencies."

Bile crept into my mouth as I remembered her hands all over me. At the police station she'd probably been trying to seduce me into staying out of the way, but this afternoon she'd known it wouldn't work and done it anyway, just for the pleasure of watching me squirm.

"But your own husband?" My voice cracked with bewilderment.

"Do you blame me? After the money and the women? And, yes, I knew about them both before you crawled your way into the light. And you know, I would have put up with it, except he was thinking of giving me up. Imagine, abandoning me for someone like that dim French slut at the Ostia."

"Why couldn't you just let him divorce you?"

Her mouth curved upward in a mockery of a smile. "And let him waltz away with my money? Never. He was going places, Mr. Dawson. He would have been mayor again, and then after that it's the state congress and then the real congress and maybe if he was very, *very* lucky he could have been more. And he would have had some other tart by his side."

"You killed him for spite? You had six people killed for *spite*?"

"I don't think of it as spite. I think of it as cleaning up a mess and starting over." She glanced at my trembling gun. "Do put that away. You're too young to play with such dangerous things." She took the pistol out of my hand while keeping her own revolver trained on my chest. "Let's make a little trade, shall we? My gun for yours. It keeps it simple for the police when they get here."

Sirens wailed in the distance. Emma had probably called the police before following us, maybe even as soon as I walked in the door. It felt like I'd been shoved underwater. Everything around me was muffled by my own pounding heart. Why hadn't I just shot her instead of asking questions? Damn my need to know. I thought about trying to run, but I knew it wouldn't work. She'd just shoot me in the back. She'd had no problem killing her own father to cover her tracks. Murdering me wouldn't even make her flinch.

Something moved in the corner of my eye. I had a blink of hope that someone was seeing this. If there was a witness, it would be harder for the police to buy whatever sob story she was going to tell. But I didn't dare take my eyes off the guns. She pulled back the hammer of her revolver. I didn't shut my eyes. I wouldn't let her see that I was scared.

Something metallic flashed in the streetlight by Emma's neck, followed by a bright squirt of blood. Her mouth opened in shock as the knife pulled away. She dropped like a stone, and the guns fell out of her hands. They made no sound as they tumbled into the muddy grass.

I gaped for a few seconds at her body. I raised my head. Sev, his shirt misbuttoned and untucked, was standing just a step away from where Emma had been, panting and holding a dripping knife. He looked terrified.

"Christ, Sev," I gasped.

He tried to smile, but it didn't quite work. "She deserved it."

Chapter Twenty-Six

I LOOKED AT Emma's body, still not quite making the connections. "But how did you know I was here..."

Sev yanked something from his pocket and brandished it at me. It was the letter I'd left on the bed for him. "You slammed the door on the way out."

My mouth moved, but nothing came out of it. The sirens screamed.

He shoved the papers back into his pocket. "We need to go. Now."

He threw the knife over the fence into the river. It made a splattering sound as the water swallowed it. Without thinking, I did the same to the borrowed gun. Emma could keep her own revolver. As far as I knew, it only had her fingerprints. That would keep it simpler for Harlow and his one-track mind. Though how he was going to explain away her gaping neck wound was anyone's guess.

Sev ran, and I followed. Everything was a blur of black and gray with the occasional patch of yellow where a functional streetlamp beamed. We avoided those, mindful of the light. After a while, he slowed and started scrutinizing our surroundings. I glanced around. I might have known where we were in the daylight, but in the dark, I had no idea.

Sev and I wandered a few blocks, staying in the deep shadows. I held my breath, waiting for some sound to indicate that we'd been seen, but the city remained silent and asleep. Even the sirens were too far away to hear now.

Just as I was about to ask him where we were supposed to be going, he pulled me into an alley. Something about it struck me as familiar, but how different was one alley from another? I thought we were just going to hide there, but Sev hammered on a door. It echoed back. I knew the sound. We were at Bella's.

"*Chi é?*" asked a voice. A panel in the top of the door I hadn't noticed before slid open, and a pair of suspicious eyes looked out.

Sev turned in profile so the scar down his cheek was visible to the guard. The eyes moved away and the panel closed again. The lock made a clunking sound as it unbolted. Sev dragged me through the door as soon as it opened.

The guard said something I didn't understand, and Sev snapped a reply. They went back and forth for a moment; then Sev shoved me toward the spiral stairs.

"Go," he said. Then he added over his shoulder, "*Trova Bella. Subito!*"

The stairs made an unholy racket as we pounded down them. At the bottom was a dark, cramped space that reeked of cigar smoke and stale alcohol. A crackling radio set right next to the door played ragtime. As my eyes adjusted, I could make out three large round tables, all surrounded by men playing cards. A pot of crinkled bills was piled at the center of each. The players looked up, glared, then went back to their games.

"What is this place?" I asked.

"Doesn't matter," Sev answered as he pushed me along. "It's private and safe."

At the far corner of the room, black mold spread in a spiderweb pattern across the wall. A small table with four matching chairs was positioned just in front of the largest splotch. A collection of empty and half-drunk bottles and glasses littered the top of it. If my skin hadn't already been crawling, it would have started to.

Sev waved at one of the chairs and took a seat in the other. He pulled out his cigarette case and took out two. He tossed me one and lit his own. His foot beat an uneven rhythm on the cement floor.

"What were you thinking?" he hissed.

"What was *I* thinking? What were *you* thinking?" I dropped my voice. "You just killed Emma Carlisle!"

"And she was going to kill you. I told you I'll protect you. Even from the police." He exhaled a mouthful of smoke. "Who was the dead man?"

"Her father. Um, Marc Logan. But she did it! She was going to frame me for it!"

A look of relief came over Sev's face. "You didn't kill him?"

"No! I...I wanted to. I was going to. He killed Donnie and Martin and all the rest. But I just... I couldn't. Then she came up and shot him in the face to keep him quiet. She masterminded the whole thing!" I tried to light the cigarette, but my hand was still shaking. "She talked Logan into killing people for...for justice or some other nice little thing, and she was just doing it to spite Carlisle for trying to leave her." I finally managed to get the flame of the lighter to take. I let the smoke rest in my lungs for a second. "That maid answered the door when I got to the house. The police will be all over me in another hour."

"No, they won't. Why do you think we're here?"

"We're hiding? But we can only hide for so long! We–"

Sev put his hand on mine. "Bella now owes us both a big favor. The people who killed Dario are dead. And we helped do that."

The realization washed over me. "But I didn't."

"They're dead, that's all she'll care about." He squeezed my hand again.

The sound of the door of the den opening and closing echoed into the basement. There were heels on the stairs, followed by more sporadic, almost skipping steps. Bella swept out of the landing, Pearl and her doll trailing after.

Bella scowled as she marched over to our table. "You had better have a good reason for making me come down here, Severo."

He stood up and kissed both her cheeks. "We have good news for you. Dario has been avenged."

All Bella's anger melted away. "*Davvero?*" she gasped. She pulled a chair out for herself and sat. "*Parla.*" She turned and called to Pearl. "*Gattina! Venire qui.*"

Pearl stopped hiding by the stairs and crawled into the last empty chair. "Hi Mr. Dawson. You don't look very good."

The kid had almost gotten me killed, but still I couldn't be mad at her. I tried to smile. "That's because I should be asleep. Shouldn't you be asleep?"

"Miss Bella said I could stay up as late as I want."

I sighed. So much for being a good mother.

Bella and Sev carried on a conversation around her in Italian. I assumed he was relating the night's events. Bella nodded and her eyes narrowed.

"I can give you money for a train tonight," she said in English. "Go to Aunt Nina and ask her to hide you. When she comes here for Dario's funeral, I'll send her back with the papers and the money." She gestured at the scar down his face. "That will make it harder, but it can be done."

"*Grazie,*" Sev whispered.

"Papers?" I asked.

Bella turned to me. "New identification. You can't keep your own name now, can you?"

So we were going to run for it. *Should have done that in the first place.*

"Are you going away, Mr. Dawson?" asked Pearl.

"Yeah," I answered, only half sure myself. "And, uh, I don't think I'm coming back."

"No!" she yelped. She jumped off the chair and into my lap. "I don't want you to go. If you and Mr. Martin are gone, who's going to take care of me?"

It burned my mouth to say it. "Bella will."

Pearl shrank into herself and wouldn't look at me. Bella's face flashed with disappointment, but she soon recovered.

"I was thinking," she said slowly, "she can't stay with me much longer." She gestured at the seedy surroundings. "This is not a good place for a child. She should go with you."

"We can't take a kid with us on the lam," I protested.

Bella shrugged. "Why not? Pick somewhere far and settle. The cops won't chase you. They won't even know who you are when I'm done with everything."

Could I really take Pearl? I would be out of my league already, trying to keep one step ahead of everything that'd happened, and having a little girl around wouldn't make it easier. She'd be better off with someone stable. Then again, was Bella and her world stable?

I looked to Sev. Surely, he'd have something to say about Pearl becoming a permanent addition to his life. He smiled. "I like children. There were always many around when we were younger." He glanced at Bella. "And Bella is right, this is not a good life to grow up with."

Well, that settled it. And hell, if Donnie could do it, so could I.

"Right then," I said. "I guess you're coming with us."

Pearl's eyes lit up. "I get to come with you?" She squealed and hugged me, then leaped down and ran between the tables in excitement. The other patrons of the speakie didn't pay any attention to her.

Bella smiled. "*Bene.* I'll send her with Nina after the funeral, then."

Sev stood and kissed her hand. "*Grazie mille*, Bella."

"*Basta.*" She shooed him away. "I think I will almost miss you." She glanced at me. "And you too, Mr. Dawson. One gets used to having people sniffing around." The beads clacked. "I advise you think up a new identity for yourselves quickly. I will need to start before you leave. It will be easier if it's something you come up with. You'll be less likely to forget. Besides," she leaned in, "you are the storyteller here, not me."

I mulled it over for a minute. We could be whoever we wanted. Well, within reason. No one would ever believe Sev and I were related; we just looked too different. In-laws then? That might work.

"Sev was married to my sister," I said, thinking out loud. "And I lived with them because I'm, well, I'm a writer, how much could I be making? Pearl's their daughter. And... There was a fire. She died and we lost everything. He won't throw me out because I'm his last link to her. Plus, Pearl would lose her favorite uncle."

Bella rolled her eyes. "So dramatic! But possible at least. People don't see lies if they don't look for them." She turned and looked at the clock above the bar. "Go. There is a train at four, and you will need to get things, I'm sure."

"Can I just ask one more favor?"

She regarded me. "What?"

"Donnie and Martin... I can't pay for the funerals, and I don't want them tossed in unmarked graves. And could you... I don't know, send someone to read something from me?" The idea of not saying goodbye was hard enough, but the prospect of either of them having an unattended funeral because I couldn't be there was horrifying.

Bella's shrewd eyes widened. Whatever she'd expected, it hadn't been that. "Fine."

"And Vern! Just... keep an eye on him. If he's ever put out of work—"

"I do not run a charity, Mr. Dawson," she snapped. But then she relaxed. "But for the man who avenged my husband, I suppose I can make an exception."

I pretended I hadn't heard the part about me being useful and kissed her hand. "I can't even begin to thank you enough."

The rosary shifted again. "One day I will have to join Dario in front of God, and I shall have to say my sins. Letting a good man die will not be one of them. *Ciao*, Mr. Dawson. We shall see each other again one day, I'm sure."

Bella ordered someone to drive Sev and me to my brownstone. I saw the door propped open, and for a moment I was afraid the police had already arrived. But no, in my rush I had conveniently left my book in the jamb, preventing it from closing.

I didn't own too many things, and most of Sev's possessions were still in the suitcases. I stuffed my notebook into my pocket, though I had to leave my busted typewriter. I left the keys for my apartment in an envelope on the old armchair for Mr. Blake. When we got wherever we were going, I would call Vern to explain what I could. Maybe he and Bella could keep each other in check.

Back in the car, Sev leaned against me, disregarding the driver. It didn't matter anyway. By dawn, we'd be different people a hundred miles away. I could still feel my heart pounding, but his weight against me gave me something else to focus on.

"Thanks for saving my life," I said. "Again. And for...everything else. I don't know how I would've..."

He smirked. "You're welcome, *caro mio*. But I would prefer if in this new life I didn't have to go chasing after you so often."

"I can't make promises."

"Maybe not. You're curious. And stubborn. And you won't leave well enough alone—"

"List *all* my flaws, why don't you?"

"They're not flaws when I love you for them."

I flushed and turned to stare out the window. Westwick passed by in flashes of streetlamps and headlights. The car passed a cemetery, and I stared at the passing fence with a sense of anticipation. Maybe I hoped Donnie's ghost would come out of the darkness to tell me I had done him proud somehow. But nothing happened, and the car continued on into the night. I sighed.

"Alex?"

I looked back at Sev. "Yeah?"

He remained silent for a few seconds, then said, "I never said I was sorry."

"For what?"

"For distracting you that night. You might have seen him before anything happened, and you could've avoided all this."

"Don't say things like that. You couldn't have known." I pulled him closer to me. "It's fine."

I wasn't sure if I was lying—how could it be fine with so many people dead?—but for the time being we were safe and together, and that was enough. It had to be enough.

We pulled up to the train station, and the driver handed us two hundreds before pulling away. I almost laughed. Sev didn't think the irony funny, and broke one to buy two tickets, two coffees, and a pack of good cigarettes. The platform was empty except for a handful of sleepy travelers and slightly less sleepy porters.

"Have you traveled much?" Sev asked as he passed me one of the coffees.

"No. Never been very far out of Westwick before, actually."

"Ah. Well, it will be an adventure, then."

A shrill whistle announced the train's approach and sent shivers down my spine. The train thundered in, then slowed, blasting steam and smoke. The conductor threw open the doors and called for boarding. Sev mounted the step, but I hesitated. It was a mean old city, but it was the only place I'd ever known. Would the next place be better? Worse?

Sev held out a hand and smiled, crow's feet crinkling in the corners of his golden eyes. "Come, *caro*. Run away with me."

How could I say no to that? I grabbed his hand and let him pull me on board. I took one last look before following him into the carriage. One day, one day I would come back and say my goodbyes properly. As soon as I was sure it was safe. Good men keep their promises.

Acknowledgements

I owe tremendous thanks to so many people:

My family, who tolerate this weird hobby of mine

My teachers, who tried and at least partially succeeded in gifting me with the knowledge and skills necessary to get this far

My friends—especially Andrea, Dash, and Tiffany—who sat through my exclamations and ramblings

My critiquers and writing buddies—particularly Allie, Jonny, and MH—who went through seemingly endless drafts to help me make this story the best it could be

My partner—also named Alex, incidentally—who has been nothing but encouraging, patient, and loving

And of course NaNoWriMo, Scribophile, PitMad, and NineStar Press. Without them there would be no book at all

About the Author

Thea McAlistair is the pseudonym of an otherwise terribly boring office worker from New Jersey. She studied archaeology, anthropology, history, architecture, and public policy, but none of those panned out, so she decided to go back to an early love—writing. She can often be found playing D&D, cooking with her partner, or muttering to herself about her latest draft.

Email: vsheridanwrites@gmail.com

Facebook: www.facebook.com/vsheridanwrites

Twitter: @vsheridanwrites

Other books by this author

Boiling Over (Coming Soon)

Also Available from NineStar Press

Connect with NineStar Press

www.ninestarpress.com

www.facebook.com/ninestarpress

www.facebook.com/groups/NineStarNiche

www.twitter.com/ninestarpress

www.tumblr.com/blog/ninestarpress

Made in the USA
Las Vegas, NV
03 July 2021